DEATH FROM THE SKY

A group of small black dots shot out of the clouds and hurtled down toward the huddled assembly of light grey warships. Tongues of flame burst from the sky. As the main formation of bombers began climbing for altitude, UB-44's deck gun pumped 20mm shells at them until its twin barrels were glowing with heat.

Another formation swept in low across the anchorage, and two Blenheim bombers peeled off towards the surfaced U-Boat. The chatter of their machine guns seemed unreal and remote until *Kapitanleutnant* Bergman saw the water splashes of the bullets coming nearer.

"Down!"

Every head ducked behind the thin splinter shield of the conning-tower. British bullets ripped into the U-Boat's steel plating. The 20mm gun hesitated in mid-voice, faltered for a moment, and then started to pump shells at the departing aircraft. Bergman hauled himself up from the deck planking. Looking aft, he saw a line of bullet holes neatly puncturing the hull plates—the fresh grey paint chipped and gouged to reveal the orange anti-rust coating beneath. Then he realized that the paint was stained with blood which dripped ominously down from the gun platform . . .

NO SURVIVORS

Edwyn Gray

PINNACLE BOOKS • **NEW YORK CITY**

NO SURVIVORS

A Pinnacle Books edition, published by special arrangement with Futura Publications, Ltd.

ISBN: 0-523-00568-7

First printing, February 1975

Printed in the United States of America

PINNACLE BOOKS, INC.
275 Madison Avenue
New York, N.Y. 10016

AUTHOR'S NOTES

The central characters in this story are wholly fictitious, as indeed are most of the incidents. However, this is a book about Germany's U-boats at war and for reasons of historical accuracy many of the subsidiary characters are real people. Some fought and died for their country. Others survived the conflict and are, happily, still alive today. I wish to make it clear, therefore, that the words and actions ascribed to these real-life officers and men of the *Kriegsmarine* are entirely the product of my own imagination and do not necessarily reflect either their characters or their political views.

These men were dedicated, professional seamen and true patriots and, although we found ourselves on opposite sides in 1939, I have a great admiration for their skills and a profound respect for their integrity. I hope they will understand and excuse my wilder flights of fancy. Any attempt to recount the story of the U-boats at war would be the poorer for their exclusion even though they only play fictitious roles in this narrative of Oberleutnant Konrad Siegfried Bergman's career as a U-boat commander.

EDWYN GRAY

CHAPTER ONE

The vertical side of the steel conning-tower, its fresh coat of *Type-M* (*Navy*) paint gleaming in the morning sunlight, looked dauntingly sheer. And as Konrad Bergman stared up at it he was reminded of the inhospitable face of the Grunnenburg, the mountain that hung like a sleeping giant over the red-tiled roof of his home in Bavaria But, unlike Vintenschloss, there was no clear stream tinkling carelessly around the base of the gaunt edifice. Here, in Kiel dockyard, it was moated by dirty harbour water scummed into circles of stagnant froth, embedded with dead strands of seaweed, splinters of wood and discarded cigarette packets.

Schneider, the Petty Officer who had guided him along the sloping gangway from the jetty to the scrubbed deck-planking of the U-boat, gestured towards a series of steel rungs. Bolted firmly into the side of the conning tower, they climbed the vertical, steel precipice to a small opening in the *Wintergarten* – the circular platform just abaft the bridge and periscope standards that contained the submarine's single 20-mm anti-aircraft gun.

'Up there, sir. The Captain is waiting. The other gentlemen arrived about five minutes ago.'

Konrad grasped the steel support with his hands while his foot felt for the bottom rung. His feelings of apprehension were strongly similar to those he had experienced on his first climb up the Grunnenburg with his stepfather when he was scarcely seven years old. The confident face looking up and urging him on, his feet probing for holes in the rock, his hands seemingly glued to their precarious holds and not daring to release their grip for fear that his feet might suddenly slip.

The veteran Petty Officer had difficulty in repressing a

grin as he watched the young *leutnant* sprawling his way up the side like an awkward fly. But Konrad made it and, hauling himself up on to the gun platform, dusted himself down, straightened his cap, and made his way forward to the bridge. His salute was punctilious and correct, proclaiming to everyone the recently acquired perfection of Academy drill.

'*Leutnant zur see* Bergman reporting aboard, sir.'

Otto Kretschmer returned the sparkling brand-new salute with casual ease.

'Welcome to *U-23*, Bergman. The other members of the Class are below having a look around. But we're casting off in a couple of minutes, so you might as well stay up here and see what's going on.'

The squeaking rasp of the block and tackle hauling the gangway clear of the U-boat's deck formed the prelude to the routine of casting off.

'Let go, for'ard springs!'

Kretschmer waited as the lines were lifted clear of the port bollard.

'All gone for'ard, sir.'

'Let go, after spring. Stand-by, motors.'

The taut steel hawser was released from its shackle and a mooring-line snaked down from the jetty to be caught expertly by a bearded rating who leaned forward precariously with one foot on the fantail and the other braced against the port propeller guard. The quarterdeck Petty Officer's arm jerked up straight.

'All gone aft, sir.'

'Let go for'ard breast – let go after breast!'

'All clear fore and aft, sir.'

Kretschmer walked over to the voicepipe.

'Obey telegraphs. Group down. Half astern starboard.'

There was a sharp tinkle from below as the telegraph repeater moved and Kretschmer carefully gauged the distance as *U-23* glided backwards away from the jetty.

'Helm, starboard 90 – steady as she goes – slow ahead both.'

The orders passed down the serpentine communications channel to the control-room and Konrad heard the monotonous repetition of each command and the varying pitch of the motors as the speed changed. It was a tricky job edging the 140 ft long submarine away from the jetty and the young officer watched every move the Captain made with concentrated attention.

The big diesel engines could not be used to go astern and all the undocking manoeuvres had to be carried out with the U-boat's electric motors. A good submarine commander reduced unnecessary or prolonged movements to a minimum in order to save draining the power from his batteries. And it was obvious that Kretschmer had the routine down to a fine art.

'Stop both! . . . Full astern starboard. Helm amidships.'

The bows swung to the right as *U-23* lost forward motion and her Captain watched anxiously as the submarine cleared the stern of the Depot Ship *Saar* by little more than six feet. He let the U-boat continue swinging under its own momentum until her rounded ballast tanks, the greater part of which were invisible below the surface of the dirty harbour water, were safely clear of the ship anchored ahead.

'Switches off. Engine clutches engage. Slow ahead both.'

There was a rheumy cough from the exhausts and the U-boat began to vibrate as the diesel engines shuddered to life. They glided slowly past the depot ship and Kretschmer exchanged a cheerful greeting with one of his flotilla mates leaning over the boat-deck rails watching them go past.

'Half ahead both.' *U-23's* skipper glanced over his shoulder to the young helmsman standing at the wheel. 'Think you can take her out, Ritter?'

The rating grinned.

'Yes, sir.'

'Carry on then. Keep the chequered buoys to starboard.

9

Steer course 2-8-0 when you've passed between the mid-channel markers. And don't forget that tide surge as you get level with Schmeisser Rock – we'll be going out on the ebb so it shouldn't be too strong this morning.'

Kretschmer stepped down from the raised grating he had chosen as his vantage point and nodded to Freischmidt, the First Officer.

'Take over, Number One. The pilot has left a course for you. Give me a shout when we're well into the Deeps.'

Freischmidt saluted and took his place on the tiny rostrum. He glanced down at the pilot's plot on the chart, checked the compass, and watched carefully as Ritter proudly guided his charge out past the Mole into the gently rolling waters of the Baltic beyond.

'Falke, get below and tell the cadets to come topsides,' Kretschmer told the Bridge runner waiting in the background. 'You'll probably find them in the wardroom with Engineer Baden.'

The sailor started down the brass ladder that connected the bridge with the interior of the U-boat and Bergman could hear his footsteps echoing back from the steel vault of the upper chamber. Then the sound vanished and all that remained was the throbbing roar of the 700 horsepower MAN diesels, the sharp hiss of the bow wave as the shark-like prow cut a passage through the water and the plaintive shrieks of the seagulls swooping in the submarine's wake searching for food.

U-23, now clear of the Mole, was plunging into the short waves blowing towards the shore under a keen north-east wind. Each succeeding mile made the motion stronger and soon a salty spume sprayed back over the bridge like a cold winter drizzle. Kiel and the low-lying mainland soon dropped beneath the horizon and although the sun had dispersed the morning mists a blue haze of burnt diesel smoke drifted astern to take its place.

Unlike the big battlewagons in which he had recently

served his apprenticeship, Konrad found the small submarine a lively sea-boat. Her fat ballast tanks made her roll violently while her lack of freeboard caused her to pitch excessively. And he soon discovered that he had to cling to a staunchion for support as she bucked and plunged like an unschooled horse.

'First time on a submarine?' Kretschmer asked.

'Not quite, sir. I visited my father's boat in 1918 when it was in drydock. I was only two years old at the time so I don't remember very much about it.'

'Your father was a U-boat man? What boat?'

'*UC-115*, sir. With the Flanders Flotilla at Zeebrugge.'

Kretschmer searched his memory. There was little he did not know about Germany's sea-wolves in the Great War and he took a certain pride in recalling their exploits.

'Let me see; *UC-115*. Wasn't she sunk by a British trap-ship sometime in March or April, 1918?'

Konrad was surprised at the Captain's knowledge. *UC-115* was scarcely a famous boat. In fact she had been ambushed and sunk on her first operational patrol.

'Yes, sir, she was lost with all hands. They say that the British machine-gunned the survivors in the water.'

'I doubt it,' Kretschmer said. 'Rescuing the enemy from the sea is admittedly not the Royal Navy's first priority – but that doesn't mean cold-blooded murder. If we ever have the misfortune to get involved in another war you will find, as a German sailor, that the British fight hard – but fair. Make sure you do the same.'

U-23's skipper stared out across the sea, apparently lost in his thoughts. Reaching into his pocket he drew out a battered crocodile-skin case, extracted a black cigar and stuck it between his lips. Cupping his hands to shield the flame from the wind, he applied a match to its tip and then, carefully and deliberately, put the charred stick back in its box.

'Is that why you applied for a place on this course at the Periscope School?'

11

'Sir?' Konrad could not follow his train of thought.

'Your father and *UC-115*. Is that why you want to become a U-boat officer? To avenge his death?'

A shout from the bridge cut short further conversation and saved Konrad from answering.

'Approaching the Aavold Deeps, sir!'

Kretschmer moved over to the echo-sounder and looked at it for a few moments. He nodded.

'Stop engines, Number One.' He flipped open the watertight lid of one of the voice-pipes. 'Baden? Where the hell are those cadets? Get them up here at the double.'

He snapped the cover back in place and paced slowly around the narrow circular deck of the bridge. Moments later Hans Kirchen's blond head appeared through the hatch. He climbed out, followed by the others.

'It's taken you long enough to answer the message I sent down ten minutes ago,' Kretschmer observed sourly.

'Sorry, sir. We didn't realize it was urgent,' Kirchen ventured.

'*Everything* on a U-boat is urgent, Herr Leutnant! When the captain makes a request you *jump*! Understand?'

It was apparent from their faces that they did and they shuffled their feet awkwardly. Even Bergman, who had not been guilty, felt himself to be included in the reprimand and for a few moments the bridge was completely silent. The engines had been shut down and the gulls had long since disappeared. Satisfied that he had made his point Kretschmer allowed his expression to soften. He smiled.

'You are probably wondering, gentlemen, why the authorities have given you the proverbial half-holiday and sent you for a trip on a U-boat on your very first day at the Periscope School. I will tell you. Life in a submarine is difficult to envisage when you are serving on board a large surface ship and the purpose of this trip is to show you what you are all letting yourselves in for. You will see the strict discipline that operates inside a U-boat — not the type of spit and polish discipline you get on a surface ship but an instant obedience that comes from understanding that the life of yourself and every one of the men aboard depends upon *you* doing your job quickly and efficiently. One tiny error, slowness in turning a wheel or pulling a lever, a single hesitation in carrying out an order, can bring death and destruction in its wake. Only by seeing a submarine at work can you appreciate what this means.'

He paused to draw on his cigar.

'Then, again, there is the appalling discomfort, the cramped conditions and the monotonous boredom of a repetitive routine, day in and day out. None of this can be taught in the classrooms of the Training School. Neither can the clammy fear you experience the first time you dive beneath the surface, the fear that you will never come up again, the terror of being trapped inside a steel coffin many fathoms down on the bottom of the ocean. Yes, you can smile,' he looked at Ulm, 'but until you have actually been inside a submerged U-boat you cannot know what you reactions will be. So it is better to find out the answer on the first day of the course rather than waste thousands of marks of Government money training you and then finding out that you won't make the grade.'

Kretschmer let his eyes travel slowly across the face of each man in turn. 'I love U-boats. And I hope you will come to love them too. But if, when we get back to Kiel, you feel that this is not the job for you it is your *duty* to tell the Commandant. There is no disgrace attached to being frightened and no one will hold you up to ridicule – least of all a U-boat man for *he* knows and understands what it means. Refusal to undertake the course at this stage will not be held against you in your reports. In fact, I would hazard a guess that, by facing squarely up to the facts and by not being afraid to tell the truth, you would receive a commendation mark for honesty. Is that all clearly understood?'

13

The cadets nodded – each convinced that Kretschmer had been addressing his four companions.

'Good. We will submerge in a few minutes and I will then take you on tour of the boat. Now get below.'

Kirchen led the way, followed by Ulm, Meyer and Vargas, with Bergman bringing up the rear. Kretschmer watched them disappearing one by one through the narrow hatch. He wondered which of them, if any, would make it successfully to the end of the course. Kirchen looked bright enough, despite his brashness and Vargas seemed a likely type. And Bergman? He certainly appeared to have the dedication necessary but what were his motives? A desire for revenge on the British for the death of his father was scarcely enough to merit command of a U-boat. In any case, Kretschmer thought, it was by no means certain that Britain would be their enemy *next* time.

'Start engines, Number One. Slow ahead both. Clear the deck and pass control below.'

As Freidschmidt carried out his orders *U-23*'s captain checked to make sure that the decks were clear*. After a last glance around the horizon to ensure that no other vessels were in sight, he pushed the red button of the diving klaxon. Its angry rasp squawked through the narrow confines of the submarine and there was a soft scuffle of feet as the crew went to their diving stations. Stepping on to the ladder he pulled the hatch cover down over his head and sealed off the sky.

'Both catches fastened,' he shouted to the First Officer and then, climbing down the brass ladder, he passed through the emptiness of the lower conning tower before closing and dogging the lower hatch in a similar manner.

Bergman's first impression of the interior of a U-boat was one of startled surprise at the brightness of the light. Some-

---

*On one occasion, during training, Kretschmer himself had been marooned on the deck of *U-35* when it was carrying out diving exercises and had been lucky to escape with only a ducking.

how he had always imagined it to be like a gloomy dank vault with dimly glowing lamps, a tomb-like silence, ghostly white faces, and an all-pervading air of dampness. Admittedly there was an unpleasant odour of stale cabbage water and diesel oil but, otherwise, *U-23* was nothing like the submarine of his imagination. The men looked tanned and healthy and went about their tasks with cheerful grins. The throbbing roar of the diesel engines, muffled though they were by the thick bulkheads and watertight doors, echoed back from the white-painted steel walls of the hull, and the only water in sight was safely inside a drinking glass on the chart table.

Not that the U-boat bore any resemblance to the clinical orderliness of a hospital operating theatre. Indeed Konrad had never seen such a maze of pipes, air lines, cables, circuits, levers, switches, gauges, equipment and gadgetry in his entire life. And all of it neatly fitted into a small oblong room measuring not more than 15 feet in length and 10 feet in breadth — the centre of which was taken up and dominated by the brass columns of the periscopes, now fully retracted and bedded into the open well in the floor. His mouth gaped open. It was obvious what was in his mind. Kretschmer grinned.

'It's all quite simple, once you've got the hang of it. By the time you finish the course you'll know every single one of those pipes as well as you know the streets of the town where you were born.'

Finding an odd corner — an almost impossible task in the crowded control room — the trainee officers settled down to watch the crew going through their routine diving drill.

'Stop engines, Number One. Go over to motors. I want a speed of four knots.'

'Stop engines!' Friedschmidt's hand moved the telegraph and the rumbling roar of the diesels suddenly cut. 'Clutches out — switches on. Group down. Half ahead both.'

The lights flickered as the circuits changed and a low hum

15

tingled through the U-boat as the electric motors began spinning. The effect was similar to riding in a car travelling over cobblestones and suddenly finding that the road surface had changed to smooth ashphalt.

'I shall want a depth of thirty feet, cox'n.'

'Thirty feet, sir.'

'Up forward periscope.'

The raising mechanism hissed softly and the squat brass tube rose up like a fakir's rope in an Indian bazaar. Kretschmer moved across to it, twisted his cap around so that the peak did not press up against the column and swung the lens through 360° to ensure that there were still no surface vessels in the diving area. It was a routine precaution on peacetime exercises.

'Test fore and aft planes, Number One.'

The orders passed back and *U-23*'s skipper depressed the periscope lens so that he could check the action of the hydroplanes that stuck out like gigantic flippers on either side of the submarine's hull.

'Hydroplanes tested and found correct, sir.'

Kretschmer acknowledged the report with a nod. He glanced at the five cadets huddled in the corner.

'We don't usually go through all this palaver every time we dive,' he explained. 'In fact, in action, I could get *U-23* under the surface within 30 seconds of hitting the klaxon. But we only collected her back from the dockyard last night and I prefer to check her out before diving. So now, gentlemen, if you're all ready, we'll go down and introduce you to some of those mermaids they told you about at the Academy.'

Bergman was aware of an unpleasant tightening in his throat. He glanced at his four companions to see their reactions. Ulm was studying the dials of the diving control panel with a forced concentration that obviously masked his inner feelings of unease while Vargas had braced himself against the after bulkhead and was examining the polish

16

of his shoes. Beads of perspiration were swelling on Meyer's forehead until, too heavy to cling to his skin, they rolled down his face. Only Kirchen looked calm and unaffected by the suspense of their first dive.

Konrad and Hans Kirchen had been through the Naval Academy at Flensburg together and Konrad had often felt slightly jealous of his class-mate's easy air of self-confidence. Kirchen's father, a Junker aristocrat of the old school, had, like Goering, been an early supporter of Hitler's National Socialist movement and he now held an important position in the Nazi hierarchy. As a result of his father's influence, Hans always had friends in the right places to drag him out of trouble when he clashed with traditional authority. Yet, despite the advantages of his family and his party connections, he remained a likeable fellow and a staunch companion. His rugged Nordic looks and shock of golden hair, allied to a fine strong body, made him more than usually attractive to women. And he was not backward in exploiting his advantage.

Bergman had not seen him since their last day at the Academy when they had been jointly awarded the Sword of Honour as the top cadets of their Term. And while he had gone on to join the battleship *Pommern* in the Baltic, Hans, according to the Fleet List, had been posted for 'Special Duties' the nature of which had not been disclosed. They had not met again until they had bumped into each other on Kiel's Central Dock station the previous evening. In the taxi on their way to the Dockyard Konrad had been able to fill in the missing gaps in Kirchen's career.

'Where did you get posted after the Academy? I saw they had you down for SD in the List – but that can mean anything these days.'

'London. I got myself a billet with the Naval Attaché as an ADC.' He lit an English cigarette, one of his favourite affectations, and blew a plume of smoke towards the roof of the old Daimler-Benz. 'It was a bloody sight better than pounding the decks of some old battle-wagon like the rest of you chaps. And those English girls!' His hands, huge as hams yet immaculately manicured, moved descriptively.

'You haven't changed,' Konrad had thought to himself. Still the same old Kirchen. He recalled the night they had spent at Schmidt's Biergarten when he and the other cadets had bet Hans that he couldn't make it with the barmaid before midnight. And the flushed grin of triumph on Kirchen's face as he groped his way back into the bar with only a minute left to go. Or, for that matter, the equally comic look of dismay on his face when he had to report to the MO three days later as a consequence of his amorous adventure.

'Well, you'll have to make do with our home-grown frauleins now,' Konrad had told him as the taxi chugged away from the traffic lights in the Tirpitzplatz. 'The English girls will have to learn to live without their picklespearer for a while. But you haven't told me why you're in Kiel. Still on SD?'

'The U-boat Course at the Periscope School,' Hans explained smugly. 'What on earth would I be doing in a godforsaken dump like this otherwise.' He wound down the window of the cab and threw the half-smoked cigarette into the road. 'Martell – my boss, the Naval Attaché in London – pulled a few strings when I told him I wanted my own U-boat. So here I am.'

Bergman's mouth turned down as he recalled the momentary pang of envy he had felt as he listened to Kirchen's story. It was always the same – just a matter of getting everything he wanted with the minimum of personal effort and the maximum of influence. For a moment he almost wished that his stepfather, Count Erich von Winderfeldt, had shown as much zest for picking a political winner as Kirchen's father had done. It was probably his own fault though. If he had gone into the Army like his half-brother Georg perhaps the Count would have been able to pull a few strings too. But, partly in deference to his mother's wishes and partly due to his own inclinations, he had chosen to go into the Navy like his father and grandfather before him.

Thinking of his father brought him back to the reality of the moment. He wondered how Wilhelm Bergman had felt the first time he had dived beneath the surface in the ill-fated *UC-115*. Had he experienced that same tightening of the throat, that same clamminess of the palms, that same unknown dread of the underwater he was feeling at this precise moment? And, more importantly, how had he felt when *UC-115*, holed and battered by the Q-ship's guns, plunged to the bottom for the last time?

For Konrad there was more at stake in this first dive than there was for anyone else on board *U-23* that day. Only when the submarine was fully submerged would he learn the truth about himself. And it was the fear of what he might discover that constricted his throat and made his hands sweat.

Hans Kirchen broke the spell. As the executive orders for diving echoed through *U-23*'s cigar-shaped hull he leaned across and whispered :

'One of my friends in Berlin told me that Kiel has some of the best knocking-shops in Germany – beats Hamburg hollow according to him. Let's go out and do the town as soon as we get a night off from the School.'

Despite his own inner anxieties Konrad could not repress a smile. Hans never changed. Here they were about to plunge beneath the sea and face the hazards of the underwater world and all he could think about was roistering around the local brothels as soon as they had a free night.

'Hydroplanes to dive. Main vents open. Take her down, cox'n.'

'Aye, sir.'

The hydroplane operators swung their spoked wheels while the dials above their heads indicated the diving angle to the watchful Kretschmer. Other hands pulled levers that

19

opened the main vents to the ballast tanks to admit a surge of sea water that would quickly destroy the submarine's positive buoyancy and take her down under the weight of water rushing into the empty compartments.

An array of coloured glass squares linked to the various flooding compartments sparkled to life and the First Officer called off each one to Kretschmer as the lights flickered to life. *U-23* tilted gently and Bergman felt ice cold hands of panic clutching his stomach. Was this what he *really* wanted to do? To dedicate his life to an unnatural existence under the surface of the sea? And for what? Honour and glory – or, perhaps, a premature death like his father. A gurgling, gasping, terrible death in an iron coffin and an uncharted grave on the ocean bottom. Fear gripped his brain.

Then, very faintly, he sensed the sound of the incoming sea cascading through the opened vents of the ballast tanks – spilling over the high steel lip like a mountain stream falling over the edge of a rock precipice. The image focussed in his mind and drove out the fear. It took him back to the old days in Bavaria when he used to sit on a patch of short grass watching the torrents gushing down the Grunnenburg as the Spring sunshine melted the snows high up on the peak. The sound comforted him and he felt suddenly at peace.

Sliding gracefully beneath the sea, *U-23* was no longer affected by the short choppy swell that had made her wallow and pitch while she was running on the surface. Even at periscope depth, a mere thirty feet down, the water was smooth and unruffled and Bergman's sense of calm reflected the smooth motion of the submerged submarine. With her ballast tanks flooded up, the sound of water roaring through the valves stopped and the gentle hum of the powerful electric motors added a soothing background to the unexpected sensation of peaceful tranquillity. The red pointer of the depth gauge fingering the 30 feet calibration was the only outward indication that the U-boat was now fully submerged and the tightness in Konrad's throat eased. He felt suddenly content.

Judging by the broad grin on Kirchen's face it was obvious that he, too, was enjoying their transition to the underwater world, as also were Ulm and Vargas. Only Meyer retained the strained expression that Konrad had noted just before *U-23* dived and it was abundantly clear that he was suffering the pangs of claustrophobia.

Kretschmer had also noticed the cadet's discomfort.

'Borsch,' he called to the Second Engineer standing at the rear of the control room, 'take Leutnant Meyer to the wardroom and give him some Schnapps while I show the others around the boat. I think he's brewing up for 'flu or something.'

There was no element of reproach in the tone of his voice and no hint of disdain because Meyer did not measure up to the requirements of the *Unterseebootflotille*. Just a gentle understanding sympathy that helped to mask the young man's fears.

'Will you follow me forward please, gentlemen. This is not an instructional tour, so I don't intend to explain anything in detail – that is a matter for your instructors. But I hope I will be able to give you some idea of what U-boat life is like.'

Kretschmer ducked through the oval opening in the transverse bulkhead forming the forward division of the control-room and led them down the length of the submarine to the bow torpedo compartment. The massive 21inch torpedo tubes dominated the confined space – their oiled and polished surfaces gleaming dully as they reflected the overhead lights.

'*U-23* is one of the small *Type IIB* boats so we only carry three tubes. The bigger boats, the *Type VII*s, which are just coming into service, have four up front and another in the stern. But this little trio will give you some idea of what it's all about.'

He launched into an elementary explanation of how the

tubes operated but Bergman scarcely listened. His eyes, however, missed nothing. Here in the forward torpedo compartment one became very conscious of being cooped up inside a submarine. The bulkheads and roof tapered down to the narrow razored bows and there was an uncomfortable sense of restriction and lack of space. The crew lived, ate and slept, in this tiny cramped world – their bunks slotted neatly between the cylinders of the spare torpedoes, an ever present reminder of their primary function – the Killers of the Deep. A table, slung by four stout chains from the piped maze of the ceiling, filled the narrow gangway between the bunks and served as desk, card table, writing top or dining area, according to the time of the day and the routine of the U-boat. And in every nook and corner, inextricably tangled with the personal belongings of its human inhabitants, were the valve controls, levers and switches, the twisting network of electrical circuits and the snaking high-pressure air pipes. These were the submarine's life-giving arteries and nerves which, like a vast human organism, connected every section of the boat to the brain of the control-room and the heart and lung mechanisms of the engine rooms.

Kretschmer led them back through another oval aperture in one of the transverse bulkheads that ribbed the submarine's internal structure. And, as they squeezed through, he pointed out the dog-catches and levers that controlled the heavy counter-weighted steel door.

'A U-boat is divided into a number of independent water-tight compartments and these doors form the seal that cuts each off from the other. In an emergency, if the boat is holed and water is coming in, it is the duty of every man to close the nearest door and secure it.' He paused for a moment to add emphasis to his words. 'Even if, by so doing, he traps himself on the *wrong* side of the door inside the flooding compartment. There is one golden rule in a U-boat. The safety of the boat and the other members of the crew are more important than a single individual's life. That is what I meant when I spoke earlier about discipline.'

The young officers remained silent. They could see the point Kretschmer was making but it was one they preferred not to think about. Only Bergman's thoughts moved on as he tried to visualize the interior of the doomed *UC-115* sinking slowly beneath the surface with the sea roaring in through a dozen gaping shell holes. Had his father, in those last horrific moments, had to take that fatal decision – to trap himself inside a flooding compartment to save others. Or, worse, to slam and dog the heavy door with the knowledge that, by doing so, he was trapping his friends and shipmates in the damaged fore-compartments in a desperate effort to give the captain time to save the stricken submarine.

They moved on, past the open area of the Petty-Officer's mess; the huddled antiseptic 'heads' with their special flushing pumps replacing the conventional chain; the hydrophone operator's tiny cabinet-sized office where trained ears could pick up and analyse underwater sounds at a distance of two miles or more on special listening equipment; the leather benches of the wardroom with the curtains pulled open to expose its sanctity to all who passed; and then on again through yet another watertight door into the control-room.

One thing's for certain, Konrad thought to himself, there's no such thing as privacy in a U-boat. Men lived and fought cheek by jowl for days and weeks on end. And, while one watch slept fitfully in its bunks squeezed in between the stores and equipment that filled every available place, an equal number of men of the duty watch were busy working only inches away from their resting companions. It was certainly no place for the misfit.

From the control-room they went aft to inspect the main engine room, where the big MAN diesels lay quiet and motionless, and then onwards towards the stern to the motor room. Here, in an atmosphere heavy with the sickly sweet odour of ozone, were the rounded cylinders of the electric motors purring softly as they propelled the U-boat beneath the sea at a steady four knots.

Their cursory tour of inspection completed, Kretschmer guided the four aspiring U-boat officers back to the control-room for the final excitement of their first underwater voyage.

'Up periscope!'

The column rose obediently and *U-23*'s captain swept the horizon through 360°. Then he snapped the periscope steering arms upright and stepped back.

'All clear up top. Down periscope.' He waited for the column to nest back into its womb. 'Stand by to surface.'

'Blow all tanks! Hydroplanes to rise.'

The hydroplane control wheels this time spun in the reverse direction and the levers operating the main vents moved to the closed position to seal off the ballast tanks. A sharp hiss of pressurized air echoed through the submarine as the blowing valves opened and the submarine angled slightly in response to the hydroplanes. The red pointers of the depth-gauge dials moved smoothly towards zero and the sudden pitching motion that followed the smoothness of their submerged running was evidence of the fact that they were once again on the surface at the mercy of wind and tide with *U-23* rolling and pitching like any normal buoyant boat.

Kretschmer had already released the dog catches of the lower hatch while the U-boat was surfacing and as her bows emerged he swarmed up the ladder into the lower conning-tower, unclipped the top hatch and threw it open. Staring upwards through the narrow circular opening Bergman could see the blue arch of the sky swinging backwards and forwards as the submarine rolled. He was quickly and unceremoniously pushed away from his vantage point by the two look-outs hurrying on deck to take up their surface stations on the bridge.

'Hands to surface stations. Transfer controls to bridge.' Otto Kretschmer's voice sounded oddly hollow as it filtered through the grill. 'Group down. Switches off. Clutches in – start main engines. Half ahead both.'

There was an explosive roar from the diesels and acrid blue smoke streamed from the exhausts. *U-23* tucked her bows down into the Baltic swell as the power came on and she heeled sharply to starboard as Kretschmer swung her in a wide circle heading back for Kiel.

Bergman hauled himself up the brass ladder to the bridge and drew a deep breath of fresh air. It smelled good.

He had faced the challenge and the victory was his. The morbid fears that had haunted him throughout his life had proved groundless and the dark doubts in his mind had been resolved. The crossroads of his career had been reached and he knew where he was going. The new-found confidence showed in his eyes and in the tight set of his mouth. Kretschmer noticed it with satisfaction.

'Alright, Bergman?'

'Yes sir – I'm fine.'

It was a banal and casual catechism, the significance of which was lost to the other men on the U-boat's bridge. But both Kretschmer and Bergman knew the deeper meaning behind the simple question and answer. It was part of the mystic bond that linked all submarine men together no matter what their nationality or their rank.

And Leutnant zur See Konrad Bergman knew that, at that moment, he had been accepted as a U-boatman.

CHAPTER TWO

Despite all the efforts of Dr Goebbel's propaganda ministry Karl Doenitz was not the most famous U-boat commander of World War I. In fact, as a submarine captain, he had been remarkably unsuccessful. Assigned to the crack Cattaro Flotilla and given command of the little 513 ton *UB-68* his underwater career was only briefly tinged with glory.

On 4 October, 1918, in a moment of bravado occasioned, no doubt, by the fact that the Kaiser's Germany was rapidly losing the war, Doenitz brought his U-boat to the surface in the Ionian Sea for an attack on a British convoy bound for Malta. The young Oberleutnant knew he was taking a risk but, with youthful enthusiasm, he had convinced himself that the Royal Navy, having weathered the main crisis of the U-boat war in the previous year, was now resting on its laurels and was no longer on its toes. As it happened Doenitz was wrong. A lookout on the sloop *Snapdragon* sighted the slim shape of *UB-68* within seconds of the submarine's arrival on the surface and the twin-funnelled escort ship heeled over in response to the helm as she dashed into the attack. Sweating stokers in the eerie red glow of the boiler-room fed the fires and foam boiled from the sloop's stern as she found her maximum speed. The forward 4-inch gun crew were already at action stations and the barrel swung towards the port bow quarter.

The counter-attack developed so quickly there was no time to take evasive action and, caught naked on the surface, Doenitz realized he was trapped. The first shells were already whining towards the submarine before the diving klaxon screamed its warning and *UB-68* lurched sharply from the concussion of a near miss. The men on the bridge struggled to squeeze down through the narrow conning-

26

tower hatch but it was too late. A 4-inch shell exploded on the forward ballast tank and there was a screech of high pressure air escaping from the punctured steel plating. Another swept away the U-boat's deck gun together with its unfortunate crew while a third erupted with a terrifying roar at the base of the conning-tower.

Shell splinters rattled against the plating like hail stones on a corrugated iron roof – a tattoo ominously interspersed with dull thuds as the red hot metal fragments found the yielding softness of a human body. Doenitz ducked instinctively as the exploding shells tore into the doomed submarine and he clung grimly to the conning-tower rail while the U-boat writhed and shuddered in its ritual death dance. His heavy sea boots slipped and slithered on the deck. The sea swirling at his feet was tinged red with blood. *UB-68* heeled violently to starboard as another shell ripped open her tortured hull and the young Oberleutnant knew he was beaten.

There was no disgrace at such an end. Doenitz and his boat had been defeated fairly and squarely in a clean fight. True, he had made an error of judgment in rising to the surface to attack a protected convoy but what U-boat captain had not been similarly guilty at one time or another in his career. And now, with his ship virtually gone, his responsibility rested with his crew. No officer enjoys the act of surrender but when duty has been nobly done there is no taint of disgrace in doing all possible to save the lives of the men entrusted to one's care. And Doenitz was realist enough to know that those who survived would live to fight another day.

So Oberleutnant Karl Doenitz ended the war in an Allied prison camp. Ignominiously, perhaps, but luckier than most of his comrades in the *Deutsche Unterseeboots Flotille*.* At least he was alive. And that for a submarine captain of either side was something of a miracle.

*515 officers and 4,894 men of the German U-boat service were lost in action during the 1914–18 war.

The post-war German Navy was an emasculated surface force, stripped of its modern battleships, deprived of its latest cruisers and forbidden by the terms of the peace treaty to retain its U-boat flotillas. Once again Doenitz was luckier than most of his fellow officers, for he was one of the élite few kept on to serve in the naval rump left to Germany by the victorious Allies. He retained his interest in underwater warfare, however, and was soon the acknowledged expert on all aspects of submarine operations. It was no surprise, therefore, when Hitler recalled him from command of the cruiser *Emden* to take over the creation and development of the new U-boat arm of the *Kriegsmarine* as Nazi Germany girded her loins for another war. And, like many of the Fuehrer's other intuitive selections, the former commander of *UB-68* proved, in the event, to be just the right man for the job.

Konrad Bergman was, of course, fully aware of Doenitz's reputation. There were few young officers in the Navy who were not. But to Konrad especially there was a mystic aura about a man who had actually commanded a U-boat in combat operations and, as he joined the other members of Course 3/36 on the parade ground for the traditional introductory speech by the Kommodore (U-boats), he tingled with excitement at the thought of seeing one of his boyhood heroes for the first time.

The original ten-man class was now reduced to nine for Meyer, Bergman's old Academy classmate, realizing that his phobia made it impossible for him to serve in submarines, had already seen the Commandant quietly that morning and had left discreetly just after breakfast. How many more, Konrad wondered, would fall by the wayside before the course was completed.

'Atten – *shun*!'

The Drill Warrant Officer's voice cracked like a pistol shot. The nine lieutenants, dressed shoulder to shoulder in single rank, snapped up straight and there was a flash of silver as the swords of the Instructor-Officers swept up to the salute. A chill wind blowing in from the Baltic and carrying with it the first hint of winter snow cut through the thin material of their summer uniforms.

Bergman experienced the anti-climax of disappointment at his first glimpse of Doenitz. The Kommodore's face contained none of the ruthless determination that his boyish romanticism had always associated with a veteran U-boat commander. On the contrary he looked gentle, almost fatherly, although his erect and alert bearing singled him out as a man accustomed to military discipline and the exercise of unquestioned authority. He took his place on a small platform draped with the Nazi flag.

'Stand at ease, gentlemen.'

Doenitz cleared his throat like a nervous schoolmaster addressing a fresh class of pupils at the beginning of a new term. He delivered the same speech to each intake of trainees but it came from the heart and, despite constant repetition, it had a ring of sincerity that evoked an immediate response from his listeners.

'The Navy represents the cream of the Fatherland's armed forces. The U-boat arm represents the cream of the Navy. A few of you will command submarines of your own one day. But most of you will be sent back to the big ships you came from. The future of each of you depends on your individual efforts to meet the standards I require. That is all gentlemen. Except . . . good luck.'

'Squad ! Atten-*shun* !'

Konrad brought his heels together with determination, indicating that he, for one, did not intend to get sent back to the big ships. He stood rigid, chest out, thumbs in line with the seams of his trousers, staring to the front, as Doenitz moved slowly down the line stopping to shake hands and exchange a few words with each man. He had almost stopped breathing by the time the Commandant introduced him.

'Leutnant Bergman, sir.'

Konrad saluted and shook the Kommodore's proffered hand. The soft eyes appraised him keenly and the kindly mouth smiled.

'Ah, yes, Bergman. You come from a U-boat family, I believe?'

'Yes, sir.'

'Excellent. I hope you will continue the family tradition. Good luck with the course.'

He moved on to shake hands with the next man in the line leaving Konrad with the vivid impression that, for the first time in his career, he had met a senior officer who not only knew he existed but also cared. It was an impression shared by every officer lined up on the parade ground. And although it had probably taken Doenitz only a few minutes to glance through their files in the Commandant's office and memorize some salient personal detail about each member of Klass 3/36 the mere fact that he had considered them important enough to do so showed that the Kommodore was unusual among the Navy's top brass. He was human.

It was not surprising, therefore, that when war finally came, these self-same men were eager to make any sacrifice demanded of them by their Flag Officer.

Georg Ulm yawned and drained his beer glass. 'Well, I'm for bed. We're slated for PT at six tomorrow morning and there's a half hour swim before we get any breakfast.'

Hans lit one of his English cigarettes. 'Anyone know the drill about night passes?'

'You're free every evening,' a senior trainee on the previous course told him from the depths of a leather armchair. 'Gates close at eleven but you can always apply for a late pass from the Commandant if you want one.'

'Well, thank Christ they don't treat us like kids at the Academy,' grinned Hans. 'I reckon we can make it back by eleven. How about a look around the town this evening?'

'We start lectures tomorrow,' Konrad objected. 'I doubt

if we'll have much time for evenings out while we're under training.'

'All the more reason why we should get out of this place tonight then,' Hans urged persuasively. 'Perhaps we'll be too tired tomorrow.'

'I've never known you to be too tired yet,' Konrad retorted.

'I think Kirchen's got the right idea,' Vargas said. 'We might not get a chance after tonight. And the beer in this damned place is as flat as hell. '

Hans stood up and ran his hand through his short blond hair in a gesture Konrad had seen many times before.

'You're out-voted, Kon. Two say yes and one says no – so you'll have to go along with the majority. Sounds just like one of Adolf's plebiscites doesn't it.' He took up a dramatic pose, frowned at his three-man audience, and flapped his hand back in a mock Nazi salute.

Vargas laughed but Konrad felt uneasy. Even in the cloistered ranks of the Navy it was becoming unsafe to mock the Nazis or poke fun at Hitler. Hans was too fond of relying on the protection of his father's position in the Party and one of these days he'd come unstuck. In any case, in common with most young men of his age, Bergman respected the Fuehrer. It was only thanks to Adolf Hitler that Germany now had U-boats for them to command. Without him the nation would still be grovelling for crumbs from the Allies. He sighed.

'All right, I'll come. But this is the last time until the course is finished.'

Kiel's restaurants, cabarets, and bars huddled like leeches round the dockyard area feeding on the sailor's money for their lifeblood. Shadowed back streets, constantly patrolled by Naval Shore Police, hit the glamourless brothels which catered to the needs of the seamen cooped up for weeks on end in the iron bowels of the fleet. Of necessity, this was the district closest to the tall barrack blocks of the dock-

31

yard. Next came an area of small bars and discreet houses frequented by the petty officers and less rowdy elements of the crews. And finally the broader streets of the city centre with brightly lit shop windows, expensive restaurants, gaudy cabarets and clanging yellow trams, where the officers spent their off-duty evenings.

By the time Konrad and Josef Vargas had steered Hans past the girls loitering in the doorways of the Munster Strasse they had worked up an enthusiastic thirst and *Willi's Bar,* on the corner of the Tirpitz Platz, looked inviting. It was discreetly lit by candles and the combination of faded red velvet and gleaming brass added to its atmosphere of decadent sensualism. They ordered Schnapps with a beer chaser and settled at a table near the tiny apron stage.

'I thought Hitler had cleaned up places like this,' said Vargas with a disdainful sneer. 'They tell me you wouldn't recognize Berlin these days.'

'And more's the pity, I say,' grumbled Hans. 'Christ, what we need is more bloody crumpet – not less. If you ask me old Adolf's ruining Germany. If we go on at this rate we'll be asking permission to wipe our noses.' He swallowed his beer gloomily, banged the empty glass on the table, and ordered another round.

'I suppose it's better than having red flags flying everywhere and OGPU offices in every town.'

Konrad disliked talking politics but Hans was needling him into retaliation. Vargas quickly rallied to his support.

'Bergman's right. Just look at what we've achieved in Germany since Hitler came to power. There's no more unemployment and the country's more prosperous than its ever been.'

'Crap!' said Hans shortly. 'If you knew some of the things I've seen when my old man has been entertaining his party friends you might not be so keen. Cleaning up Germany?' He gave a sharp laugh. 'They ought to start cleaning themselves up first.' Kirchen took a mouthful of schnapps. 'You know, Josef, you sound just like one of those brown-shirted morons who spend their time sieg-heiling at the Nuremburg rallies.'

Vargas's face flushed. 'I'm not ashamed to admit that I'm a member of the Party. And if I had my way every officer in the Navy would be too.'

'I suppose *you* are, as well,' Hans asked turning to Konrad.

'As it happens – no, I'm not. I'm not interested in politics and I don't think the Navy should get mixed up in these things. But you have to admit that Hitler has done a lot of good for Germany and he deserves our support whether we're in the Party or not.'

The mingling of good beer and strong spirits was beginning to make Bergman's head swim. He hated talking politics and Hans's disrespect for authority made him feel uncomfortable. The bar was getting hot and stuffy and his hand was unsteady as he put his empty glass back on the table.

'Let's change the subject. I thought we'd come out to enjoy a drink. And in any case it's time we were getting back to barracks.'

'Agreed, but we must have one more for the road. I was just getting warmed up.' Hans called the waiter across and ordered another round. 'My solemn promise, Kon. One last drink and then you can take me home and tuck me into bed.'

Vargas was considerably drunker than either of his companions. His face was red and he was swaying in his chair. He slopped beer on the tablecloth as he raised the *stein* to his lips. Putting the glass down he slumped forward on his elbows and stared across the room.

'That sort of thing makes me mad,' he slurred. 'Bloody Jew bastard mauling a German girl about.' He started to rise from his chair but the effort was too much and he fell back awkwardly.

Hans followed the direction of Josef's eyes. 'You mean the

chap with the bald head and the girl with the big tits?'

'Thas' right,' Vargas agreed. He let out a substantial belch. 'Chap with the bald tits and the big head — bloody Jew bastard.'

Konrad looked at Hans anxiously.

'Let's get him out of here before he creates a scene,' he said, getting to his feet.

Kirchen stood up and came round to the other side of the chair. Taking hold of one arm each, they lifted Vargas up and guided his weaving feet across the crowded room to the exit. It was not a prepossessing sight and Bergman felt guiltily conscious of his blue naval uniform as they pushed through the tables. Kirchen seemed blissfully unaware of the sour looks they were getting but they made Konrad feel uncomfortable. The night air was refreshingly cool and as they emerged into the street he felt his head clearing. They propped Josef up against a convenient wall, choosing a discreetly dark corner to hide their purpose, and waited while their companion was sick.

'It's my fault,' Hans admitted as he took out one of his English cigarettes and lit it, 'I should have remembered the stupid clot can't hold his liquor.'

Vargas reappeared from the shadows. His face was ashen and his legs unsteady. Hans caught him as he lurched forward and pushed him back against the wall.

'Pull yourself together,' he snapped. 'We've only twenty minutes left to be back in barracks *and* we've got to get you past the SPs on the gates.'

Vargas slid slowly and ungracefully down the wall as his legs buckled beneath him. He began to sing. Kirchen's open hand struck his cheek hard. Josef shook his head, braced his hands back against the bricks, and pushed himself upright.

'That's better,' Hans said.

'Sorry — God, I feel terrible.'

Kirchen gripped his arm, wheeled him round to face the

downward slope of the hill and got him moving. As they started walking he glanced at Konrad.

'You were always better at night navigation than me, Kon. What's our quickest way back?'

Bergman stopped for a moment to get his bearings. 'I think if we turn down here,' he said indicating Tannenburg Strasse, 'and keep going north we should come out somewhere near the main gates.' He nodded at the moon rising above the roofs. 'If we keep the moon on our left we ought to be on course.'

They turned down Tannenburg Strasse. It was part of old Kiel with dingy shops, now locked and shuttered for the night, and flat-fronted terraced houses that opened straight on to the pavement. Hans walked along the kerb, supporting Vargas as he lurched unsteadily, while Konrad kept his eyes open for street names that might confirm they were heading in the correct direction.

'How long have we got?' asked Hans.

Konrad checked his watch. 'Twelve minutes.'

Turning left into another equally dingy street so that the moon remained roughly on their left they quickened their pace. Vargas, revived by the cool night air, was now more steady on his feet, though he still had a tendency to weave.

Suddenly a short distance ahead they heard the sound of breaking glass, the scream of a frightened woman, and angry shouts. Leaving Vargas to follow under his own steam Kirchen and Bergman hurried forward. The street narrowed to an alley and then emerged into another. Almost directly on the corner was a small delicatessen shop. Broken glass from its shattered window lay strewn over the pavement and two men wearing brownshirt uniforms and black leather jackboots were helping themselves to an assortment of sausages, salami, and cold meats. The proprietor, a middle-aged man wearing a white apron was grappling with a third storm-trooper while a woman crouched in the doorway with her face in her hands.

One of the SA men* looting the window turned to join his companion, dragged the man back against the wall, and hit him hard. The white apron stained red as the blood ran down from his mouth. Then the stormtroopers took it in turn to hit him.

'Bloody Jew!'

Mostovitz went down on his knees as the fists pounded him. A heavy boot thudded into his ribs. The woman looked up and began screaming again.

Hans stopped, took in the squalid scene at a glance and turned to Bergman.

'Come on, Kon. Let's break it up.'

He started across the street at a run. Konrad hesitated. He had witnessed similar scenes before and, like the majority of Germans, he had usually looked the other way. It was not good policy to tangle with Nazi thugs when they were Jew-baiting and he could not afford to fall foul of the Party at this vital time in his career. But if he didn't give Hans his support they'd kill him. With a quick backward glance to see whether Vargas was still safely following on behind he ran towards the shop.

Hans had a punch that complemented his big frame. And he used it with obvious relish on the stormtrooper who had kicked the delicatessen proprietor. A short hard left into the soft paunch immediately above the eagle-badged belt fastener followed by a straight right to the face sent the brownshirt bully reeling back into the shattered window. His head struck the marble display counter and he rolled over unconscious in a pile of smoked sausages.

The second man leapt for Kirchen but Konrad was in time to haul him off and drive a balled fist into his mouth. The stormtrooper staggered under the punch and then returned to the attack with flailing arms. Bergman halted him with

*Footnote: Sturmabteilungen (Stormtroopers) — the Nazi Party's original quasi-military supporters who wore the notorious brownshirt uniform.

a parried left and hit him again. As he moved in to follow up his advantage he saw Hans haul the third Nazi up by the collar and plant his foot firmly into the well-upholstered brown breeches. His victim screamed as he slithered face forward into the broken glass littering the pavement.

Konrad sank down on to one knee as his opponent kicked out hard and he raised an arm instinctively as the SA thug prepared to follow it up with another aimed at his face. But the intention was never realized. Hans spun the stormtrooper round, steadied him with one hand, and then smashed a pulverising fist into his face dropping him to the gutter like a slaughtered ox.

He was grinning all over his face as he helped Konrad back to his feet.

'I enjoyed that. Are you okay, Kon?'

Bergman dusted the dirt from his trousers and wiped a smear of blood from his lips. He was still too winded from the jackbooted kick to answer.

'Thank you, my friends,' Mostovitz said quietly. 'But now you must get away from here quickly . . . the police will be along soon and it is not good they should find two officers of the Navy mixed up in such things. Quickly, my friends.'

Almost before the warning was finished there was a blast of whistles from the direction of Tannenburg Strasse and shouts of 'Polizei! Polizei!' Hans looked at Konrad. Instinctively they grabbed Vargas who was still swaying aimlessly on the kerb, his eyes staring in puzzlement at the body of the unconscious stormtrooper sprawled in the gutter, and dragged him in the direction of the dockyard.

'There'll be bloody hell to pay over this,' said Bergman suddenly aghast at what they had done. 'Why the hell couldn't you leave it alone like everyone else does?'

Hans broke into a half-run and Vargas stumbled as his two companions urged him along.

'You know damn well why I couldn't – any more than you could have done. Only *you* won't admit it. The recriminations can come later. Right now we've got to get this stupid bastard through the gates without the provost smelling him a mile away. *And*,' he added darkly, 'let's hope he was too drunk to see what happened.'

Bergman stopped dead without warning and Hans just caught Vargas in time to prevent him from falling into the gutter.

'*Now* what?' Kirchen demanded.

'My cap . . . I must have lost it in the fight.'

'Well we can't go back for it now; the place will be swarming with police. For Christ's sake come on, Kon. *Hurry up.*'

It was a stroke of fortune that their arrival coincided with two truckloads of ratings who had sampled Kiel's wide range of wine and women rather too well and too deeply. The Duty Shore Patrol descended on the singing seamen like pirahna fish swooping on raw meat and in the ensuing confusion Vargas was smuggled through the gates undetected. They carried him up to their rooms on the second floor of Block B just as the *Lights Out* bugle call echoed through the barracks. And then, having got him undressed and into bed, they retired to Kirchen's room for a night-cap.

'God, you look a sight,' Hans observed dispassionately when he saw the dried blood on Konrad's face and the darkening bruise under his right eye.

'Oh, to hell with my looks, Bergman snapped angrily. 'What am I going to say if they find my cap and report me to the Commandant? I'll be lucky to escape a court-martial. And it's all *your* bloody fault,' he added bitterly.

Hans passed him a glass and lay back on the bed. 'You didn't *have* to come wading in,' he pointed out. 'I could have handled those three on my own – those SA bully boys are easy meat.'

'It's all very well for you,' Konrad stung back. 'But I don't happen to have a father who can pull Party strings and get me out of trouble.'

Kirchen lit a cigarette and blew a neat smoke ring towards the ceiling. 'Take it easy, Kon. You won't need anyone pulling strings for a caper like this. What *you* ought to be worrying about is our friend Vargas. If he was sober enough to remember what happened you're going to need more than strings. Don't forget he's a Party member.'

'What do you mean – *I'm* going to need more than strings. What about you?'

Hans put his cigarette down in the ashtray, took Konrad's glass, and smiled easily. 'Well it's *your* cap they'll find – not mine. Good night, old boy, and sweet dreams. Perhaps it will never happen.'

But at three o'clock the following afternoon it did.

Klass 3/36 were just leaving the lecture room after an introductory talk on the theory of hydrodynamics when a Chief Petty Officer bustled importantly down the corridor.

'Leutnant Bergman?'

'Yes, Chief? I'm Bergman.'

The CPO saluted. 'Compliments of the Commandant, sir, and he'd like to see you in his office immediately. And Leutnant Vargas as well, sir.'

Konrad seethed inwardly. Himself and Josef. How the hell had Hans managed to wriggle out of it. The bruise on his cheek flamed darkly in anger and his mood was not helped by Kirchen's soothing 'Good luck, old boy, better watch out for Vargas,' as he followed the Warrant Officer down the corridor.

The Commandant's office was austerely furnished and the tight-lipped expression on Kapitan Grosse's face added no warmth to the uninvitingly chill atmosphere. Bergman saw two Stormtroopers standing to one side of the massive mahogany desk and he experienced a momentary glow of satisfaction at the marks of damage on their faces. Then he saw his naval cap with its white cover ripped and torn lying on the desk in front of the Kommandant and his heart sank.

Vargas, his face still pale from the previous night's debauch, joined him and together they came to attention and saluted.

'Were you two in the Hoffmann Allee last night at about 10.30?' Grosse asked. Konrad decided to act as spokesman.

'Yes sir.'

'And is this your cap, Leutnant Bergman?'

'It is, sir.'

The Kapitan placed his hands together, his fingertips touching in a judicial attitude. It was obvious that he was not enjoying the interview.

'Gruppenfuehrer Horstmann tells me that he and two of his friends were brutally assaulted by two naval officers last night in the Hoffmann Alee. What do you have to say?'

Konrad suddenly remembered a ruse he and Hans had once used to get out of trouble in their Academy days when they had got themselves involved in a fight with some local High School students. It was pushing his luck but it was worth a try.

'I'm afraid the Gruppenfuehrer has his facts slightly wrong, sir,' he said quietly. 'There was a great deal of confusion and it was dark. I did not attack the Gruppenfuehrer. I was trying to assist him, sir.'

'*Assist* me!' exploded Horstmann.

'Please do not interrupt,' Kapitan Grosse warned sharply. 'I have listened to your account of the – er – incident. Now kindly let us hear Bergman out. You may continue, Herr Leutnant.'

'It was like this, sir. A bunch of communists were attacking the stormtrooper – there were four or five of them at least – and I thought they needed naval support. So we joined in but, in the darkness and confusion, things got a bit mixed up. The communists must have slipped away when they saw us arriving and the Gruppenfuehrer thought we were part of the gang.' He shrugged. 'It developed into a free-fight all round.'

'Why did you run away afterwards?' demanded Horstmann with a gleam of triumph in the eye that was not puffed up and bruised where Hans' fist had found its target.

'I must apologise on that score, Herr Gruppenfuehrer, but the Kapitan-Kommandant will understand. It was almost time for the Barrack gates to be closed and we had to obey standing orders to be back by 11 o'clock as we had not applied for late passes. I felt that our duty under the Naval Discipline regulations outweighed our civil responsibilities. On reflection I realize we were wrong, sir. But no doubt you will understand and appreciate our dilemma.'

Kapitan Grosse made no comment. He looked at Josef.

'Can you confirm this account, Leutnant Vargas?'

'. . . er . . . not exactly, sir.'

'You mean Bergman is not telling the truth?'

'No, sir . . . I mean, I don't know, sir.'

The Kommandant sighed. 'Very well, Herr Leutnant, let us take matters in chronological order. Were you in the Hoffmann Allee at 10.30 last night?'

'I'm not sure, sir.'

'What do you mean – you're not sure? Were you or were you not with Bergman in the Hoffmann Allee last night?'

'I think I must have been, sir.'

'What were you doing there?'

Vargas hesitated and Konrad held his breath with anticipation. He had fought a valiant rearguard action but he knew he could not rely on a member of the Party backing up such a cock-and-bull story. Josef looked down at the carpet shamefaced.

'I – I was being sick, sir.'

Kapitan Grosse managed to hide his smile behind the clasped hands. The Gruppenfuehrer, however, could restrain himself no longer.

'There was another officer, Herr Kommandant. A tall man with blond hair.' He gestured at Vargas. 'I do not remember seeing this one at all.'

The Kommandant nodded. 'Yes, a tall man with blond hair. I think I know who you mean, Herr Gruppenfuehrer.' He pressed the button of his desk intercom. 'Tell Leutnant Kirchen to report to me at once.'

There was a grim silence in the room as they waited. Konrad knew he had been lucky over Vargas' lapse of memory but he felt more unsure when it came to Hans. With his notorious aptitude for wriggling out of trouble Kirchen was the last person in the world to rely on. What a bloody mess! There was a sharp tap on the door and in response to the Kommandant's curt invitation Hans entered the room and saluted. Konrad did not dare look at him and he stared woodenly at the oil portrait of Tirpitz hanging on the wall behind Kapitan Grosse's head.

'Were you in the Hoffmann Allee with Bergman and Vargas last night, Leutnant?'

'Yes, sir. We were returning to barracks. It's a short cut.'

'Will you give us your version of this fight?'

Here comes the crunch, thought Konrad. If Hans tells a different story to mine the game's up.

'Of course, Herr Kapitan. It was like this. We saw these three stormtroopers being beaten up by a gang of Jews so, naturally, we sailed in to help them out. I was just about to hit one of these Jewish thugs when the Gruppenfuehrer, who was obviously rather dazed, turned round and threw a punch at me. So I hit him back. After that everyone seemed to be hitting everyone else and I'm not sure what happened.'

'You say they were Jews, Kirchen. Leutnant Bergman said they were communists.'

'There's really no difference, sir,' Hans explained innocently. 'So far as I'm concerned one is as bad as the other.' He seized his opportunity to mock the SA man. 'In any case there were so many of them I daresay there was probably some of each. I mean,' he added disarmingly, 'had there only been two or three involved there would have been no need for us to go to the assistance of the Gruppenfuehrer and his men. He could have coped with them quite easily without our help.'

Horstmann opened his mouth to speak but, thinking better of it, he closed it again. Kapitan Grosse nodded.

'This really does seem to have been an unfortunate matter of mistaken identity, Herr Grupperfuehrer. I'm sure that with so many assailants it was difficult for you to see what was happening.'

Horstmann wanted to point out that the only Jew present had been Mostovitz but he somehow felt that, by doing so, it might show him up in a bad light. And in any case since a dawn visit by the Gestapo the unfortunate shop-proprietor was no longer available as a witness. He knew when he was beaten although he acknowledged it with bad grace.

'I accept the apologies, Herr Kommandant. The matter can be regarded as closed.'

But Grosse was not content to let the matter rest there. Like most senior officers of the regular Navy he disapproved of both the Nazis and their methods. And an opportunity to rub salt into the wound did not present itself that often.

'I agree, Herr Gruppenfuehrer. But I think you should thank these two young officers for having saved you from this mob.'

It hurt but Horstmann mumbled his thanks. Then, with a flamboyant Nazi salute, he stalked out of the Kommandant's office.

Kapitan Grosse stood up as the door closed. He looked at the three officers in disapproving silence for a few moments. Then his eyes twinkled.

'Whilst I appreciate your obvious loyalties to the Party, gentlemen, I hope you will not find it necessary to go to its assistance too often.' He turned and stared out of the window. Bergman could not see the Kommandant's face but there was no mistaking the veiled note of warning in his voice as he concluded the interview. 'You will find that the men of the SA are well able to take care of themselves without the assistance of the Navy. You would be advised to bear this in mind in the future. I would suggest that, while your strategy is commendable, your tactics leave a lot to be desired.'

CHAPTER THREE

16-00. Light drizzle and low cloud. Visibility poor. Wind Force 6. Trimmed to 10 metres. No ships in patrol area.

Bergman took over the first Dog Watch with customary punctuality, timing his arrival in the control room to coincide precisely with the final stroke of eight bells. The recently acquired second ring on his sleeve denoting the rank of *Oberleutnant zur See* gleamed like new gold above its tarnished and weatherworn twin. He read the deck-log, entered his name as First Officer of the Watch, and checked the chart.

'What course, *Steuermann*?'

'Steering 1-8-0, sir.'

'Good – keep it at that.' He turned to Wilhelm Mosel, the Second Officer. 'What's the met. report?'

'Glass is falling fast. I reckon we're in for a storm later on.'

Bergman grinned. 'Well you've got the Middle Watch, Willi. I shall be snugged up in my bunk while you're top-sides. I'll try to think of you – if I can keep awake.'

He studied the round white dial of the depth gauge for a few moments. Then he turned away abruptly.

'Any signal from BDU* yet?'

'Not so far as I know. If we have, the Old Man's kept quiet about it.'

UB-16 was sailing under sealed orders and both officers were equally anxious to discover what BDU had in store for them. The international situation when they had left Wilhelmshaven was not exactly encouraging and it was obvious from the preparations being made that war was

*Befehlshaber der Unterseeboote=Commander-in-Chief, U-boats.

45

more than a remote possibility. Their skipper, Kapitan-leutnant Stohr, had been summoned to attend a secret conference at U-boat Headquarters four days ago but so far he had not chosen to reveal the nature of his briefing, although he had shown them the sealed envelope containing their War Orders before locking it in the safe.

They knew, however, that *UB-16* was carrying the new magnetic mines in place of her normal outfit of torpedoes. And the knowledge brought Bergman small comfort. Very few submariners enjoy being closeted with a cargo of mines but, for the officers, the dangers were compounded by frustration for, without torpedoes, they had no means of underwater attack. And deprived of their main attack weapon there was little chance of winning the honour and glory of which they dreamed.

'Up periscope!'

Obergefreiter Dorfmann, the man responsible for operating the raising mechanism, thrust the lever down firmly in obedience to Bergman's order. The periscope moved upwards and Konrad gripped the handles before it had completed its full ascent. *UB-16* was fitted with the old-type 'scope with guidance handles and his left hand moved like a motor-cyclist revving his engine to tilt the periscope eye upwards towards the sky. He swept round the full 360° to check for aircraft and then, moving his hand forward, dropped the lens into the horizontal position to survey the horizon. Pushing the handles back to their upright 'rest' position he stepped back.

'Down periscope.'

Willi was still hovering in the control room. He lowered his voice so that the men on duty watch could not hear.

'Do you think it's war, Bergman?'

'Your guess is as good as mine, Willi, Konrad shrugged. 'I'm sure the Fuehrer will do all he can to avoid it but you can't trust the British. Last I heard was that Chamberlain was flying to Munich for discussions. Don't worry, we'll soon know if the balloon goes up.'

'I suppose so. It's this hanging about that I hate. The British have probably got us pin-pointed already and the moment they get the word they'll send in their destroyers to blast us to kingdom come with their depth-charges.'

'Don't be so bloody morbid,' said Konrad. 'I'm more concerned that we aren't kitted up with torpedoes. I wonder what damn fool at HQ dreams up the brilliant idea of sending the U-boats into battle without weapons. I don't know the full score but I've heard that Prien's *U-47* and Otto Kretschmer's *U-23* are carrying mines too. So is *UB-7*. What a waste!'

'*UB-7*? Isn't that Hans Kirchen's boat?'

'Yes,' said Bergman curtly. He was still seething at the unfairness of the whole thing. Not that he wasn't still friendly with Hans. It was just that Hans had been given a command before he had – despite passing out of the Periscope School three places lower.

Willi lowered his voice confidentially. 'I did hear a rumour that Kirchen was given a boat on the Fuehrer's personal orders. Nice to have influence, eh?'

'Up periscope.'

It was the only way Bergman could work off his uncharacteristic surge of temper and keep Mosel quiet. He pulled the handles down, took a routine sweep of the sky and then twisted the left-hand grip to search the horizon. He swept through the first ninety degrees, hesitated, continued around the full circle, and returned to the starboard beam sector. Two masts peeped over the horizon rim. He brought the high-power attack lens into position and the two masts stood out starkly against the sky as the telescopic lens magnified the image. He could see the cross-trees plainly on both masts and the tiny detail immediately identified the hull-down vessel as a surface warship.

'Captain to control room!'

Bergman checked the bearing and called off the estimated range, course and speed of the mystery man-of-war to Mosel who fed the data into the *Torpedorechner* – the Attack Table on which the trigonometrical problems of torpedo deflection angles were resolved by means of mechanical calculations to ensure the correct amount of 'aim-off' on firing. It was, of course, a waste of time, for *UB-16* was not carrying her torpedoes but it was good practice.

'Down periscope. Steady as she is, *steureman.*'

Kapitanleutnant Stohr hurried into the control-room, his uniform jacket unfastened, his hair touselled, and his eyes still hooded with sleep. But, despite appearances, he was already wide awake and alert.

'Warship bearing Red 70, sir. Unidentified. Range approximately eight miles.'

Stohr nodded.

'Up periscope.'

He began buttoning his jacket as the column rose up from the deck. 'Don't look so jumpy, Bergman. We're not at war yet, you know.'

Putting his eye close to the monocular lens of the viewfinder he carefully studied the unsuspecting ship cruising peacefully in the distance. Konrad could see the pin-point of light reflecting down the tube into Stohr's eye. It was their sole contact with the surface world above. Only the captain knew what was going on up there and, for the first time, Bergman suddenly realized how much their lives depended on that little circle of light and the skill of the man who was priviliged to look into it.

'Down periscope.' Stohr turned to the hydrophone operator. 'Range report, please.'

'Six miles and closing, sir. HE* suggests a destroyer.'

UB-16's skipper rubbed his chin reflectively. 'She was a bit closer when I looked, Number One. And we're on converging courses. Looked like one of the British *Tribal*-class

*Hydrophone effect.

destroyers.' He paced across the narrow width of the control room, turned when he reached the bulkhead and paced back again. 'Why the hell did they send us out without torpedoes? Even if we get the War Warning Signal right now there's damn all we can do about it.'

'Couldn't we surface and signal her position, sir? The Luftwaffe could pick her up inside twenty minutes and a Stuka Squadron could blast her out of the water with ease.'

'We *could*, Number One. The only trouble is we've been forbidden to break radio silence because of these damn mines.'

He moved back to the periscope but, after a moment's hesitation, decided against using it.

'Group up. Full ahead both. Bring me on to 1-3-5, helmsman.'

UB-16 increased to her maximum speed of 7 knots – submarines, when running submerged, are not exactly underwater greyhounds – and Konrad could feel the vibrating power of the motors crescendo like an orchestra responding to its conductor.

'Hydrophone report, please.'

'Four miles and closing, sir.'

Stohr glanced at the Patent Log and then looked up at the brass-rimmed chronometer. 'She's doing all of thirty knots, Number One. Must be relying on speed to keep her out of potential trouble. I had heard they can't use their ASDIC* at anything more than twenty knots so they probably don't know we're around. I wonder if it's true?'

'Why not find out, sir?'

'How, Number One?'

'Well let's assume that they're on war alert like us – and I can't picture the Royal Navy kicking its heels when

---

*The Royal Navy's top-secret U-boat underwater detection device developed between the wars. It took its name from the initials of the Anti-Submarine Detection Committee responsible for its invention.

there's the chance of a fight at any moment. If we show ourselves for a few seconds and then dive again quickly it's going to make them feel a bit jittery. You know the sort of thing I mean — "Are those German swine going to attack us without waiting for war to be declared?" '

'I'm glad you've got an imagination, Bergman,' Stohr observed drily. 'Still, it's certainly an idea. We might even get some useful intelligence for BDU.' He thought for a moment. 'I think it's worth trying — providing, of course, that their lookouts are on the ball. If they don't see us it'll be a wasted exercise.'

Konrad remembered his father. 'Don't worry about that, sir. *They'll* see us all right. The British always seem to know when there's a U-boat around.'

The periscope glided upwards in response to the sharp click of Stohr's fingers and *UB-16's* skipper took a last quick survey of the surface situation.

'Down periscope. Stand by to surface. Keep her on motors — we won't have time to connect and disconnect the main engine clutches.'

Bergman's routine commands put Stohr's order into execution.

'All vents closed. Hydroplanes to rise. Blow all tanks.' He watched the tell-tale lights of the trim indicator as *UB-16* angled towards the surface.

'Christ! Jock, there's a bloody U-boat coming up!' Able Seamen Murray, Port Bridge-wing lookout of HMS *Viking* wanted to rub his eyes to make sure he wasn't seeing things. Restraining the impulse he shouted his warning to the bridge.

'Submarine! Two miles off port bow.'

Commander St John Powers swung his binoculars in the direction given by Murray.

'He's right, Number One. Obviously doesn't know we're around or he wouldn't dare show his ugly face.'

'It's definitely German, sir. I can see the net cutters up front on the bows.'

'I know what it is, Number One. I was hunting U-boats while you were still wetting your bed.' He bent over the voice-pipe. 'Radio cabin? Are you sure there's been no War Signal from the Admiralty?'

'Yes, sir. Nothing since five o'clock and you've seen that one.'

Lieutenant Digby-Moreton continued to watch the surfaced submarine through his glasses. 'Must have seen us, sir. She's diving.'

Commander Power's eyes narrowed briefly as he made his decision.

'Reduce to half speed. Steer 1-5-0. Depthcharge crews close up.'

Viking heeled over as the helmsman swung the wheel on to the new course and the bow wave frothing under her stem fell away as the destroyer lost speed.

'ASDIC on. Track and hold.'

The Commander was enjoying the thrill of the hunt. It brought back memories of his midshipman days operating out of Queenstown in 1918.

'Depth-charge detail secured, sir.'

'Set fuses for 50 feet and remove safety pins.'

'Are we going to attack, sir?'

Powers shot a scathing look back at the Sub-Lieutenant hovering at the rear of the bridge. 'Of course not, you bloody fool. We're not at war – *yet*.' A slow smile spread over his face. 'But, by God, if we receive the Admiralty signal while we've got this bastard in our sights I'm sure of one thing. We're going to sink the first U-boat of the war.'

'ASDIC contact, sir.'

'Where?'

'Bearing Green 0-7-0. Speed about three knots. Depth fifty feet.'

PING-PING . . . PING-PING . . . PING-PING.

The sharp single echoes of the probing Asdic beam sounded like the pips of a radio time-signal as they bounced off *UB-16*'s hull. Stohr glanced at Bergman with a sour smile on his face.

'You seem to have been right, Herr Leutnant. They've picked us up on their damned box of tricks almost immediately. So, as it was your idea, you can have the honour of deciding the next move.'

'Let's lie doggo for a while, sir. Then we could try some rapid course changes to see if they can hold us when we start wriggling.'

'And then?'

Konrad had it all worked out. 'We go deep and see how far down they can chase us. There must be *some* limit to their depth-ranging.'

'HE approaching. Bearing 0-8-0. Estimated speed 15 knots.'

They didn't need the hydrophone operator's report. The drumming beat of the destroyer's engines were clearly audible inside the steel drum of the control-room.

'Stop motors,' Stohr ordered. 'Maintain absolute silence.'

The hum of the electric motors faded away and an eerie silence descended on the submarine.

PING . . . PING . . . PING . . . PING.

'We've learned one thing,' *UB-16*'s commander whispered to Konrad. 'She was doing a good thirty knots when I saw her. Now she's dropped away to around half speed. So it looks as if their detection device won't operate at maximum speed.'

The thump of the destroyer's engines crescendoed to a roar. It was an unnerving sound even though, lying submerged at 50 feet, they were quite safe from the dangers of collision.

'HE very close. Bearing 0-8-5. Speed 15 knots.'

PING ... PING ... PING ... PING.

HMS *Viking* was right overhead and the monotonous high-pitched pulses suddenly faded and died. The thundering noise was now immediately above their heads and Bergman could scarcely conceal his elation.

'They've lost us, sir.'

Stohr put a warning finger to his lips.

'HE passed overhead. Bearing now 2-6-5. Speed still 15 knots.

PING ... PING ... PING ... PING.

'Sorry, sir. I spoke too soon.' Konrad looked puzzled. 'How did they pick us up again so quickly?'

Stohr shrugged. 'I'm not sure. All I can imagine is that the device won't work when the ship is directly above a submarine. If I'm right that's the second thing we've learned. You realize what it means if my conclusions are correct?'

'Yes, sir. If a U-boat can move directly beneath the hunter maintaining an identical course and speed with the surface ship the ASDIC won't be able to pick it up.'

The engine noises had now ceased to be audible except on the U-boat's sensitive hydrophones and Stohr needed the help of his own detection devices before planning their next move.

'Situation report, please.'

'Speed still 15 knots but HE bearing changing. Probably turning.'

The monotonous metallic pulses faded away as the distance passed beyond the Asdic's range and *UB-16* prepared to escape the net.

'Switches on. Group down ... half ahead both. Course 0-1-5.'

The U-boat turned through 90° and groped forward like a blind fish at five knots.

'Approaching last contact zone, sir.'

Commander Powers nodded and hunched forward over

the bridge rails, as if expecting his eyes to work better than the detection devices. The ASDIC repeater behind his head pinged steadily but the double echo, the sound that indicated a positive contact, was missing.

'Passing over last point of positive contact now, sir.'

'Thank you, pilot.'

Which way had the U-boat gone? A wrong decision now and the Hun would have escaped. It was moments like these that made Powers wish the responsibility wasn't his. He took a gamble.

'Steer 3-6-0.'

'Three-six-zero it is, sir.'

'Number One – any signals yet?'

'No sir. Intercepted message from Captain (D) to *Hotspur* but nothing from the Admiralty.'

'I suppose that bloody fool Chamberlain's having tea with Adolf again and he won't tell us there's a war on until he's finished the washing-up. Tell me, Number One. How did Nelson get away with disobeying orders? Didn't he attack the Danish fleet at Copenhagen before war was declared?'

PING . . . PING . . . PING-PING . . . PING-PING.

'Got him, by God!' Powers grinned in triumph. 'Now let's hold the bastard until we get the word to start shooting.'

There was less jubilation in the control room of *UB-16*. Stohr and Bergman exchanged meaningful looks as they heard the pulses start again. It was time to put the next stage of Konrad's cat-and-mouse plan into action.

Take her to 100 feet. Stay trimmed for two minutes and then flood down to 125 feet.'

The red pointers fell away and settled gently at the 100 feet calibration but the pulses followed relentlessly. 125 feet did not shake off their electronic shadower. And neither did 150 feet although Konrad felt sure the pulses were weakening in strength. They seemed to be trapped as neatly and effectively as a fly in a spider's web.

'What do you think, Bergman? I'd say the sounds were getting weaker each time we go deeper.'

'So would I, sir. In fact I'm certain we could dive completely out of range. Another fifty feet could well do it.'

'Perhaps – but the old *UB-16*'s not as sprightly as she was. The last Dockyard report shows her tested only to 25 fathoms. Another fifty feet would take us into the danger zone.'

Bergman understood Stohr's hesitation. Every submarine has a safe diving limit beyond which the hull structure may be too weak to withstand the increased pressure of the sea. To venture below that limit was to court disaster for the power of the sea was quite capable of crushing the U-boat's shell like a giant squeezing a chicken's egg. But, even so, there were occasions when a captain had to take such a calculated risk, when he had to weigh the odds between the power of the sea and the menace of the enemy on the surface. And this, in his opinion, was such an occasion.

'I'd say we've *got* to break contact, sir. War might be declared at any moment and when it does that British destroyer has got us full in its sights.'

'We are not at war yet, Herr Leutnant. And until we are I don't intend to hazard my boat. If the War Signal comes through we'll go deeper and take our chance. But until then I will rely on course and speed changes to confuse the tracking devices.'

'With respect, sir, if war breaks out we won't know anything about it until the first depth-bombs go off. While we're pinned down below periscope depth we can't pick up radio signals – but the British, being on the surface, *can*. BDU can send us as many signals as he likes but we won't be able to pick up a single one of them. We've got to go deeper.'

Stohr did not like being corrected but he was shrewd enough to listen to advice. And there was something about Bergman that commanded attention. He rubbed his chin. The relentless *pings* were like some hideous torture from an

Edgar Allan Poe horror story. They made him feel edgy and uncomfortable. But the young Oberleutnant seemed unaffected and Stohr envied his calm precise reasoning under stress. There was no question about it. By the time a man got to forty he was too old to command a U-boat. Leave that to the youngsters.

'How old are you, Bergman?'

'Twenty-two, sir. Why?'

'No reason, just curiosity.' He smiled wearily to himself and turned to the men at the diving control panel. 'Take her down to 200 feet, Cox'n.'

Mannheim had been listening to the conversation. He hoped the Old Man knew what he was doing. His stoic expression gave no hint of his inner qualms.

'200 feet, sir.'

UB-16 edged further into the depths, her plates groaning under the increased pressure, the men inside staring upwards anxiously as they watched the roof for tell-tale leaks indicating a sprung rivet. The ASDIC echoes had ceased and an oppressive silence settled over the interior of the U-boat.

Bergman walked across to the deck log, picked up a pencil and made a brief entry :

30 September, 1938. 1850 hrs. Hunted by destroyer. Dived to 200 feet. ASDIC echoes ceased. Hull sound. No leaks. KB. (O/L z.s.)

'Most Immediate signal, sir.'

Commander Powers took the slip of paper from the Yeoman of Signals. 'I suppose that now we've lost contact on the ASDIC Jolly Roger* is going to tell us there's a war on.' He glanced down at the message :

Captain (D) to Viking. 1847 hrs. Negative (repeat) negative hostilities. Come home for tea the toast is getting cold.

*Admiral Sir Roger Backhouse was First Sea Lord from 7 September, 1938 to 15 July, 1939.

Powers balled the signal form and threw it over the side. His monosyllabic expletive – manifestly impossible with a shipload of males aboard – helped to relieve his frustration. He looked suddenly weary from the hunt.

'Take over, Number One. And stand down the depth-charge crew. Anyone would think there was a bloody war on! He stalked off the bridge.

Bergman glanced at his watch.

'We've been down an hour, sir.'

Stohr stirred himself out of his reverie. 'Take her up to 100 feet, cox'n, and hold her trimmed.'

The twin bronze propellers turned lazily as they strained against the pressure of the sea and the controls responded sluggishly. *UB-16* lifted slowly at first and then more quickly as the propellers began to bite. She stopped rising at 100 feet and every ear strained to pick up the ASDIC pulses. But they had gone. And the lack of sound was almost as unnerving as the previous menace of the probing echoes.

'Perhaps they've lost us,' Stohr mused aloud. 'Or perhaps they want us to surface so they can finish us off with their guns.'

Bergman had a sudden vision of an identical scene in *UC-115* on that fateful morning in January, 1918. The Q-ship lurking on the surface, her poop low in the water where the torpedo had blown a hole in her stern, her gun-crews lying hidden behind her masked weapons waiting for the U-boat to show herself. Had Kirkheim, *UC--115*'s skipper, faced the same dilemma as Stohr? A strange inner voice warned Konrad that he was repeating his father's words.

'There's only one way to find out, sir.'

UB-16's commander nodded. 'Agreed, Number One. But we don't know the situation. If we come up to the surface we've got to let them fire the first shot because *they* know if war has been declared and we don't. Perhaps I'm getting too old and cautious but I prefer to cross my bridges one at a time. Take her up to 30 feet, cox'n.'

UB-16 glided upwards, levelled out, and held trim as ordered.

'Up periscope.'

Stohr closed against the eye-piece as Dorfmann pulled the lever.

'Any HE?'

The hydrophone operator, his ears gloved with heavy padded receivers, shook his head.

'Not a sound, sir.'

The periscope broke surface and, as the water drained from the lens, Stohr peered anxiously like a one-eyed Cyclops. The others waited tensely wondering what would happen next. Dorfmaann, the eternal optimist, was quite sure there was nothing in sight. Willi Mosel, with youthful enthusiasm, waited expectantly for the order to fire torpedoes – and then kicked himself for forgetting that *UB-16* wasn't carrying any. But of all the men penned inside the square steel walls of the control room Bergman endured the worst torment. With memories of *UC-115* vivid in his mind he could already hear the sharp crack of the destroyer's 4.7-inch guns and the sickening thud of exploding shells. Outwardly he was calm and composed. Inwardly his stomach churned with anticipation.

Stohr stood back from the eye-piece with the air of a man hearing a last minute reprieve in the death cell.

'Stand by to surface, Number One.'

The compressed air hissed through the submarine as the pressure forced the sea-water ballast from the buoyancy tanks and *UB-16* emerged on the surface in a bubble of white froth with the sea streaming from the drain-holes ribbed along her waterline. Stohr unclipped the lower hatch as she broke surface, clambered up the ladder and unfastened the clips of the upper hatch. As he heard the water draining he threw the hatch cover upwards and hauled himself on deck.

'Look-outs on deck,' he yelled down through the circular opening. 'Switch over to main engines. Transfer control to bridge.'

'Switches off – clutches in. Half speed ahead both. Obey bridge orders.'

The vast fans began to whirl, sucking the fresh sea air down inside the submarine, and there was a belching roar from the diesels as *Leutnant (Ing.)* Lufte coupled the clutches and started the main engines.

'Signal from BDU, sir.'

Bergman took the slip from the telegraphist and hurried up to the bridge. Stohr read the message quickly and handed it back to his First Officer.

1925/30/9/38. From BDU Stop to Commanding Officers afloat Stop All units return to base with utmost despatch Stop exercises completed stop.

'So that's why the Royal Navy let us get away,' Konrad said quietly. 'There's no war after all. The Fuehrer has achieved victory without a single German soldier or sailor shedding blood.'

Stohr did not reply. He stood silently with his elbows resting on the curved ridge of the conning-tower coaming deep in thought. Suddenly he straightened up and walked over to the voicepipe.

'Send Mosel up to take over the Watch.' He turned to Bergman. 'Let's go to the wardroom, Number One. I'd like to find out what's been going on while we've been playing cat-and-mouse with that destroyer.'

Pausing in the control room to give the Navigator details of their revised course Stohr moved on into the open area designated as the wardroom. He pulled a heavy curtain across for privacy and lifted a small battery wireless down from one of the overhead lockers.

'Let's see what the BBC have to say.'

'But surely it is forbidden . . .' Bergman began to protest. Stohr silenced him with an impatient gesture and twiddled the knobs in search of the London transmitter.

'Listening to British radio stations is an approved procedure for obtaining intelligence. If you don't believe me look it up in the book – para 165 or 166.'

Konrad didn't believe him but he was not disposed to argue. Radio stations meant naval transmitters *not* propaganda broadcasts beamed to a gullible world by the BBC. It was not the first time he had seen a veteran officer show a similar cynical disregard for official instructions when it suited him and it offended his inborn sense of dutiful discipline.

There was a lot of static interference and, even when Stohr finally located the BBC on the medium waveband, the broadcast was disjointed and only came through in sections. But both men recognised the quavery tones of Britain's Prime Minister, Neville Chamberlain :

'This morning I had another talk with the German Chancellor, Herr Hitler. Here is the paper which bears his name as well as mine. I would . . . read . . .' His voice faded unintelligibly amid the atmospherics and Stohr turned the knob impatiently. '. . . and the Anglo-German Naval agreement as symbolic of our two peoples never to go to war with one another again. We are resolved . . .' Bergman's ears strained to pick up the words and Stohr cursed as a slow morse signal came in over the top and drowned out all other sound. '. . . Bring with me peace in our time . . .' A burst of teutonic martial music effectively jammed further reception and *UB-16*'s captain gave up.

'Thank God for that,' he said solemnly.

Bergman agreed – but for different reasons.

'We should thank the Fuehrer for saving the Fatherland, sir. We're nowhere near ready for war yet and he knows it. But he's beaten the warmongers by diplomacy and given us more time. Just wait until we get the Z-plan ships* built. Then we'll show 'em.'

*A complete construction plan for increasing the size of the German Navy to parity with Britain by 1944.

Stohr sat back on the leather settee and threw his cap on to the small table in front of him.

'I won't disagree with you, Number One, because you're still young and enthusiastic. But I shall be 40 next month and I'm due to be posted out of U-boats at Christmas. Even if they decide to keep me on I shall only be given a shore-appointment somewhere. What I meant was — thank God *I* won't be at sea when war finally comes. For mark my words, Konrad, it *will* come. And when it does it will be the young men of your generation who will have to fight it. And God help you.'

'Don't worry, sir. *We'll* fight. And next time we'll *win*.' There was still a trace of boyish enthusiasm in Bergman's confident grin. 'I only hope they wait until I've got my own U-boat to command.'

CHAPTER FOUR

Neville Chamberlain's sanguine hopes for 'peace in our time' were not reflected in the martial activities of the Nazi Government nor, for that matter, in the hasty preparations of its British counterpart. Both would-be protagonists, suddenly aware how close they had been to the brink of war, redoubled their industrial and military efforts in readiness for the inevitable conflict. And Hitler, taking advantage of a carefully engineered escape clause in the Anglo-German Naval Agreement, announced in December, 1938, that he intended to increase his U-boat fleet to parity with the Royal Navy's seventy-strong submarine service.

Guided by the *Kriegsmarine's* Commander-in-Chief, Admiral Erich Raeder, the Fuehrer was well aware of the truth contained in the former's advice to him in 1935 that 'The key to German power at sea lies below the surface. Give us submarines and we shall have the teeth to attack.' Indeed, Hitler had observed, when he handed Raeder details of the submarine clauses in the Treaty, 'There are your teeth.'

The Admiral could recognize von Ribbentrop's machiavellian hand in the tortuous wording of the agreement and especially in the proviso that Germany could build up to parity with the Royal Navy if 'a situation arose which in their (Germany's) opinion made it necessary'. The British ignored the threat posed by the loophole. After their victory over the U-boats in 1917, the invention of ASDIC, and their vastly improved anti-submarine weapons, they complacently considered that the U-boat threat had been licked. So, even if Hitler could field a fleet of seventy submarines, the Admiralty felt sure that they would have little or no effect on their lines of sea communications. It was an error of judgement that was to cost Britain dear in the months to come.

Kapitanleutnant Stohr was an early casualty in the new naval race. Trained U-boat commanders were in short supply and his fond dreams of retirement were abruptly shattered by the frantic submarine construction programme. For Bergman, however, the political developments brought fresh hopes of an early command. The increasing flow of commissioned U-boats meant an urgent demand for new captains and, with his seniority and experience, there could be little doubt that he would soon receive the appointment on which he had set his heart.

But the gratification of mere personal ambition was not his only reason for satisfaction. Like Raeder, he considered the U-boat the Navy's most effective weapon against England's oceanic empire. And he saw, too, an opportunity to avenge his father's death and, at the same time, a chance for the Navy to atone for its part in Germany's defeat in 1918. To wipe out such a national humiliation was a cause for which he would willingly sacrifice his life. And his feelings were shared by the majority of Germany's young naval officers.

Kommodore Karl Doenitz, patriot though he was, had long since outgrown such schoolboy sentiments. For him the coming war meant a life-and-death struggle for the survival of the Fatherland. And despite the bragging boasts of Goering and his Luftwaffe he knew that he alone held the key to Germany's victory in his U-boats.

The U-boat Command Buildings in Wilhelmshaven were, as usual, a hive of activity. His coffee, cold in its cup, lay forgotten on the desk as he read and signed the various papers laid before him by his secretaries. Then, having completed his day-to-day routine work, he picked up a small bundle of report sheets in readiness for his favourite task – the selection of the Navy's future U-boat commanders.

He passed over the first two rapidly – approving one and

rejecting the other. But the next file aroused his interest and he leaned back in his chair to read it slowly.

CURRENT REPORT ON OBERLEUTNANT ZUR SEE KONRAD SIEGFRIED BERGMAN, FIRST OFFICER UB-*16*. PERIOD 1 AUGUST, 1938 TO 31 JULY, 1939.

CONFIDENTIAL

Oberleutnant Bergman had acted as First Officer throughout my period of command. He has undoubted qualities of leadership and is liked and respected by the crew. A first-rate officer in every department, amenable to discipline, but able to act on his own initiative.

His reactions under active service conditions in September, 1938, are already the subject of my report AK/1/12/10/38. As a result of his judgement I was able to obtain certain intelligence on British ASDIC defences which has proved of great use.

Well bred and of good appearance. An excellent comrade. Has a character of the highest integrity. While still full of youthful enthusiasm he is mature enough to avoid rashness.

(a) Suitable for what position?   *U-Boat command.*

(b) Suitable for promotion?   *Yes, to Kapitanleutnant.*

(c) Potential further promotion?   *Korvetenkapitan at least.*

(Signed) M. F. Stohr. Kapitanleutnant.

Recommendations approved. (Signed) Walther.
Kapitan z.s. OC 10th Flotilla.

Doenitz put the Report form down on his desk and glanced through the earlier appraisals tucked inside the file. The award of the Sword of Honour at the Academy was recommendation in itself and *Pommern's* captain praised him but 'thought that he would be better suited to the initiatives required on small ships than the disciplines of battleships'. The Kommodore smiled as he read the spidery comment. He knew von Pau of old and the terse phrase spoke volumes. He picked up the blue graduation report from the Periscope School and nodded. Then, leaning back in his chair, he closed his eyes and searched his prodigious memory for a recollection of the man whose future career now rested on his decision.

The date of the Graduation Report helped to pin-point the occasion and the scene on the windswept parade ground of the Periscope School slowly focussed in his mind. The line of anxious young lieutenants eager to impress and aglow with enthusiasm on their first day in the U-boat service. Mentally Doenitz ran through the faces he had stared into as he exchanged salutes and shook hands with each man in turn. Yes, now he had him. Medium height and slimly built. Dark hair and firm clear eyes. He recalled the eyes well. There was a certain expression in them that indicated the confidence needed to command. As the mental picture clarified he recalled their brief conversation.

The Kommodore leaned forward and opened his eyes. This was the young man whose father had been killed in a U-boat during the war and who had made such an impression on Kretschmer. Good material there. Good solid traditional material – and, by God, the *Kriegsmarine* needed that type of tradition. He picked up his pen and in his bold angular script he annotated the bottom of the buff report form :

Approved for command. (Signed) Doenitz. Kommodore. BDU.

Then, placing the green folder in the wire tray on the left hand side of his desk he reached for the next file.

August, 1939, was a month of heady excitement for Oberleutnant Konrad Bergman. Rumours of war were whispered in every wardroom and there was an urgent atmosphere of bustle and hurry to prepare the ships and men of the *Kriegsmarine* for the impending conflict. Hans Kirchen had told him over a drink at the Helmsdorff Hotel that every available Panzer Division was moving east and the roads of East Prussia, where he had just spent his summer leave, were clogged with army vehicles. Snatches of conversation he had picked up in his father's office in Berlin had convinced him that Hitler was about to strike at Russia.

When Bergman returned to *UB-44* that evening he turned out the charts of the Baltic and began studying them. If war with Russia was about to start he intended to know the probable area of operations like the back of his hand. The bottom of the sea was his battlefield. And every good general surveyed the ground before a fight.

Then, on 22 August, came the bombshell news of the Russo-German non-aggression pact and Hitler's unexpected *rapprochement* with Stalin. Yet the tanks and troops continued to roll east and war seemed closer than ever. Konrad, like many of his countrymen, felt bewildered by these sudden shifts in the diplomatic chess-game and, while Hans took a Lufthansa ticket back to Berlin to see the latest in his never-ended stream of girlfriends, Bergman decided he would be better employed getting his boat into combat condition so that he could respond immediately to any calls made upon him. The higher direction of the nation's foreign policy was not for him. He was a simple career sailor with a job to do. And the sooner he concentrated his entire attention on the job in hand the better.

UB-44 was tied up at Pier G and Konrad returned the salute of the Watch Officer as he climbed aboard. *UB-44* was one of the latest *Type-VIIB* submarines built by the Germania Werft at Kiel and she was not due to celebrate her first birthday for another two months. Her surface displacement measured 753 tons and, when trimmed for diving, she took on just over another hundred tons of sea water as ballast. She was 218 feet 3 inches in length from the tip of her bows to the farthest point of her stern where it tapered over the twin bronze propellers. Her beam was a fraction over 20 feet at its maximum but her side-slung ballast tanks took up most of this. There was no place inside her cigar-shaped hull that measured more than 16 feet across and, even then, the intricate maze of machinery and controls that festooned her bulkheads effectively reduced the free space by at least six feet. But, cramped or not, Bergman would not have exchanged her for the biggest battleship in the Navy.

Despite her diminutive size she was a fully-fledged fighting ship with a 3.5-inch quick-firer on her forecasing and a 20mm anti-aircraft pom-pom on a railed platform abaft the conning tower. And her outfit of twelve 21-inch torpedoes made her a lethal match for any surface ship afloat.*

As the last days of August ticked away Bergman obtained permission from the Flotilla Commander to take *UB-44* out on a short shake-down cruise and the following afternoon he was putting the crew through their paces off Wilhelmshaven.

'Captain to the bridge!'

Bergman put his coffee cup down on the wardroom table, grabbed his white-sleeved cap † and hurried up through the control room to the ladder leading to the bridge. Despite the fans whirring below to keep the atmosphere fresh there was a pleasant biting tang to the sea air as he emerged through the circular hatch-opening.

'Two large warships bearing 1-8-5, sir.'

Raising his Zeiss binoculars he watched the light grey warships approaching from the south.

'*Graf Spee* and *Scheer*,' he nodded as he focused on the angular single-funnelled pocket-battleships steaming five miles on the starboard quarter. 'You should have called me up earlier, Bauer. You know my standing orders. I am to

---

*The *Type-VIIB* U-boats were powered by 2,800 bhp MAN diesel engines giving a surface speed of 17 knots. For underwater cruising they relied on 750 shp electric motors yielding a maximum submerged speed of 8 knots for ten hours. Each submarine carried five torpedo tubes – four in the bows and one in the stern.

†It was a tradition in the U-boat service that only the captain wore a white cover on his uniform cap.

be called *immediately* any warship is sighted. And any means *any*.'

'Sorry, sir. But as I knew they were ours I thought it would be all right.'

UB-44's captain continued to watch the sleek armoured ships coming up from astern and he made no effort to conceal his admiration for the ingenuity that had gone into their construction. Limited to a maximum displacement of 10,000 tons by the penal clauses of the peace treaty, German designers had set out to produce armoured battleships within the confines of a cruiser's tonnage.* By the use of electric welding for the hulls and diesel engines for propulsion the *Panzerschiffes* carried a devastating armament of six 11-inch guns in two triple turrets plus a secondary armament of eight 5.9-inch guns plus numerous anti-aircraft weapons. The heavy guns meant that they could crush anything smaller than a battleship while their speed, 26 knots, enabled them to run away from any enemy ship heavy enough to defeat them.

They were the ideal commerce raiders and that was the role the German Naval High Command allocated to them. And their range of 19,000 miles meant that they could operate on far-flung missions calculated to stretch the British Navy's defensive resources to the limit.

Bergman altered course towards them. His keen eyes noted that they were riding low in the water and were obviously fully stored and bunkered. It did not need much prescience to guess that they were on their way out into the Atlantic where they would be able to disappear in the ocean's vast grey wastes safe from the prying eyes of the Royal Navy until war actually began. He wondered when he would – even *if* he would – see them again. And on impulse he called *UB-44*'s crew up on deck to witness their imposing passage.

*It was established after the war that the so-called 'pocket-battle-ships' exceeded the Treaty tonnages by 20% and in fact displaced 12,100 tons.

As the two *Panzerschiffes* swept past with high white bow waves at the base of their straight stems Konrad rested his binoculars on the conning-tower coaming.

'Zermer,' he called across to the Yeoman signaller standing on the port side of the bridge nearest the two surface ships, 'send a signal – "Good luck. Leave some for the U-boats." '

Zermer cradled the six-inch signal lamp in the crook of his left arm while his fingers clicked a rapid tattoo on the trigger. There was a pause and all eyes watched the signalling bridge of the *Graf Spee* waiting for the reply. Suddenly a shuttered searchlight began winking and Zermer read off the flashes :

'Thank you. Long Live the Third Reich. Heil Hitler.'

'I bet Langsdorff didn't dictate *that* reply,' Bergman thought to himself. *Graf Spee's* captain was an officer of the old school – a first-rate seaman, a humane fighter and a patriot. The type of man who would be proud to say 'Germany' and to have gloried in the name. He smiled to himself as he imagined Langdorff's sour expression when he read the *Graf Spee's* signal log later that day.

UB-44 was now running on a parallel reverse course to the two big ships and, raising his cap, Bergman led his men in three rousing cheers for each battleship as they passed.

'Hoche! Hoche! Hoche! – Hoche! Hoche! Hoche!'

The theatrical gesture of patriotic fervour did the men good – making them feel part of a greater whole dedicated to the defence of the Fatherland. And Konrad firmly believed in the psychological necessity of such demonstrations.

UB-44's Nazi ensign dipped in salute and there was an answering cheer from the men lining the rails of the two pocket-battleships. Then they were past and driving on to the misty rim of the horizon, leaving behind only the oily fumes of their diesel exhausts. The excitement over, Bergman sent the men below, gave the helmsman a change of course for Wilhelmshaven and remained on the bridge to enjoy the air.

Fifteen minutes later a third black smudge grew over the horizon and resolved slowly into another of the *Panzerschiffes*.

'Well, it must be either *Koenig* or *Deutschland*,' said Bauer. 'We've only got four and the other two are already hull-down to the north.'

UB-44's skipper nodded his agreement. 'Let's see who has the best pair of eyes, Number One. A free drink at the Helmsdorff tonight for the one who identifies her first.'

Bauer grinned. 'You're on, sir.'

The pocket-battleship was closing at high speed, presenting herself at an awkward bow angle that made identification difficult, if not impossible, even to an expert.

'It's the *Koenig*,' Bergman said decisively.

Bauer kept his binoculars glued to his eyes and the distance closed by more than another mile before he felt confident enough to give a tentative nod of assent. Even then he wasn't entirely sure.

'She's certainly got a lighter control-tower than *Scheer* and *Spee*, but that applies to both *Koenig* and *Deutschland*.' He stared through his glasses again. 'You win, sir. I can see the catapult abaft the funnel — and I know *Deutschland* carries her spotter-plane up front of the stack.'

'I see you know the official recognition features, Number One. But you'll need to be sharper than that when we get into action.'

Baur admitted defeat with a rueful grin. 'It was the angle she came at us, sir. Completely masked the catapult and I couldn't see it properly until we changed course.'

'At least you've learned one lesson today, Number One. *And* an important one at that.' He turned to Zermer. 'Call her up and ask "What ship?" ' As the Signaller lifted his lamp Bergman turned back to Bauer. 'The official recognition charts are based on broadside silhouettes — which is all very well if the other ship conveniently shows you her beam. But how many times does that happen in practice? I realized this almost the first time I looked through a periscope. So when I was in Berlin last year I bought a lot of scale model ships and produced a series of my own silhouettes showing all world's major warships viewed from awkward angles. And it taught me to identify by means of odd details they never mention at Training School. *Koenig,* for example, has two bridge wings, whereas the other ships of her class all have three. It's not so obvious when you see her broadside-on but, on the bow quarter or from astern, they stand out like a showgirl's tits and it's easy.'

Zermer, the hand-lamp tucked under his arm, was standing at his side.

'Reply from *Koenig,* sir.'

'Go ahead.'

The Warrant Signaller hesitated. Then he decided to take the plunge. 'Signal reads, *"Whose dat down there saying whose dat up there?"* ' He coughed apologetically. 'At least I *think* that's what he replied, sir.'

Bergman smiled. Meyer, the young officer who had dropped out of the U-boat course because of claustrophobia, was *Koenig's* signal's officer and they had been term mates at the Academy as cadets. Johann's collection of American jazz records was always something of a standing joke amongst his contemporaries and Konrad recognized the title.

'Reply to *Koenig* : "Hands up or I'll shoot." '

'You've got a nerve,' thought Zermer but his lamp clicked obediently. There was an immediate answering blink of light.

'From *Koenig,* sir. Message reads, *"Not, repeat not, understood."* '

Bergman swallowed hard as he realized that the second reply had been transmitted from the big 10-inch lamp on the Captain's bridge. Evidently someone with four gold rings on his sleeve was eavesdropping. He pushed the button of the klaxon diving alarm with his thumb.

'Reply to *Koenig* : *"Auf Wiedersen."* '

It was a stage exit that, for audacity, equalled that of the Royal Navy captain who dipped the funnels of his steam-driven submarine in salute to Admiral Beatty in the latter days of 1918. And Konrad could picture the expression on von Mikel's face as the U-boat slid beneath the surface. *Koenig's* commander was not renowned for his sense of humour.

Watching the scene from the lower signal bridge of the pocket-battleship Johann Meyer suddenly envied Bergman's ability to dive out of trouble. The wrath of a four-ringed Post Kapitan could be a terrible thing to witness and there were times when he wished he had a similar ability to cock a snook at von Mikel and then vanish.

Six hours later *UB-44* nosed her way into Jade Bay, swung to starboard as she rounded the Six Fathom Marker Buoy and gently eased into her berthing position alongside Pier G. A veteran *Oberbootsmann* was waiting for Bergman as he came up the gangway.

'The Kommodore wants you in the office immediately, sir.'

Konrad's heart sank. Surely von Mikel had not signalled a complaint about his behaviour to BDU. It was the sort of bloody-minded thing he would do.

'I have a staff car waiting at the entrance, sir.'

Bergman nodded and followed the Chief Petty Officer along the wooden planking of the pier. He noticed an armed sentry on guard at the entrance and felt sure he hadn't been there when they had left the previous day. But he was too concerned with his own problems to give the new security precautions much thought. He returned the sentry's salute and, with the same feeling of apprehension he had experienced when summoned to the Kommandant's office after the punch-up with the three SA men in Kiel, he climbed into a small grey-painted Opel Kadet.

'What's it all about, Chief?' he asked, as Herzog bounced the little car over the dockyard railway track.

'Couldn't rightly say, sir. The brass don't usually confide in CPOs. But there's a hell of a flap on. Haven't you heard the news?'

'Christ!' thought Bergman, 'Don't say von Mikel has complained direct to OKM.'* The old bastard could always claim that *UB-44*'s sudden dive had hazarded his ship. And although Konrad knew that he had steered *away* from the pocket battleship on submerging his sudden exit must have caused considerable concern on *Koenig's* bridge.

'We haven't heard any news for some time, Chief,' Herzog said.

'*UB-44* was on a shake-down exercise and we were running deep for over four hours. And you can't pick up radio signals below 30 feet. What's happened then?'

'We invaded Poland early this morning. The Panzers have broken right through and Goering's boys have plastered Warsaw into rubble. We're at war, sir!'

The Opel pulled up outside U-Boat Headquarters with a squeal of brakes and Bergman adjusted his cap carefully before getting out. The armed guards at the sandbagged entrance demanded his papers brusquely and then, having examined them, saluted respectfully.

'This way, *Herr Oberleutnant*. The *Kommodore* is expecting you.'

Konrad followed the *feldwebel* along a green-painted corridor and found himself ushered into a sparse office manned by an elderly *Kapitan* and two equally elderly female typists. The former checked his papers, flicked the switch on an ancient Telefunken internal telephone, and announced his arrival. A metallic grunt assented with a curt '*Kommen sie.*'

Bergman removed his cap, placed it under his arm and went into the *Kommodore's* office, coming smartly to attention in front of the desk. Doenitz looked up. The dark rings

Oberkommando der Kriegsmarine – Supreme Naval Command.

under his eyes showed that he had been working without respite all through the night.

'At ease, Bergman. Take a seat. Don't look so nervous.' His eyes creased in a smile. 'You will find that I make a habit of chatting informally with my commanders, whenever I can.' He pushed a silver cigarette box across the desk.

'Thank you, sir; I don't smoke.'

Doenitz raised his eyebrows. 'I wish you could persuade Kretschmer to adopt your abstemious habit. I'm sure he sometimes comes to the surface just so he can light a cigar.' He laughed. 'But as he is one of my best U-boat commanders I suppose I shouldn't grumble over such a minor indulgence.'

Bergman felt at a loss for words. It was scarcely the sort of chit-chat conversation he had envisaged having with his Commander-in-Chief on the first day of war.

'You will have received the War Signal, of course,' Doenitz continued, without any perceptible change in the tone of his voice.

'No, Herr Kommodore. *UB-44* was running submerged for about four hours, so we were under DR* condition.'

The U-Boat Chief frowned and studied the signal log lying on his desk. 'But Headquarters have been transmitting the War Signal every hour since 0600. At what time did you surface?'

'At 0715, *Herr Kommodore*. We passed the duty picket patrol-boat just before 0755 and as, we were in visual signalling range, and in accordance with Standing Orders, we shut down the radio. No war message was received from the Port War Signal Station – only confirmation of our berthing position.'

'All right, Bergman. I believe you,' Doenitz agreed. 'If I thought you were the type to miss a signal I would never have recommended you for command.' He dismissed the matter with a shrug, although his pencil scribbled a reminder to include the PWSS as a repeater station for priority signals

*Dead Radio.

in future. 'Berlin has little doubt that England and France will be at war with us in a matter of days and most of the flotillas are already under Battle Readiness Orders.'

Bergman's heart raced at the thought of being in action at last. He had seen seventeen of the big *Type-VII* boats leave for their war stations on 19 August with a further six of the small coastal U-Boats following eight days later. But *UB-44*'s battery problems had kept him tied up to Pier G until leaving on the shake-down cruise the previous day. And, sensing that something big was in the wind, he had felt sure that he was being left behind while his friends had all the fun.

Doenitz stood up, walked across to the wall safe, pulled it open, and drew out an envelope sealed with uneven dabs of red wax. He handed the packet to *UB-44*'s skipper.

'Here are your sealed orders, Bergman. You will be advised by radio when to open them. How soon can you get to sea?'

'Four hours, sir. *UB-44* has been fully provisioned for the last month. We only need to ship warheads from the torpedo store and top up the fuel tanks.'

'Good.' The *Kommodore* glanced at a small leather-cased travelling clock on his desk. 'I want your boat to leave at 1400 hours. I need not remind you that all U-Boat officers and men are subject to a Condition One security alert. No communications are allowed with either friends or relatives until the position is clarified. And remember that at the moment we are at war only with Poland, so you must curb your natural enthusiasm if you meet up with the Royal Navy.'

He offered his hand and Bergman took it in a firm grasp.

'Good luck, *Oberleutnant*.'

'Thank you, *Herr Kommodore*.'

Bergman saluted and left the austerely furnished room. As he walked out of the Headquarters building he touched his hand against the bulge of the secret orders in his breast pocket. It was stupidly romantic, he knew, but he felt at least two inches taller. Herzog opened the door of the Opel and he climbed in. They jolted over the cobblestones of the old dockyard in silence for half a mile before Konrad returned to earth.

'Tell me, Chief, why are you on a shore job? We could do with men like you at sea at a time like this.'

'Too old, sir. I was just nineteen when I joined the U-Boat service in 1912 – work it out for yourself.' The *Oberbootsmann's* crumpled face disintegrated even further as he grinned with cheerful resignation. 'So last year they called me off *U-47* – Prien's boat – and put me on this job.' His eyes looked wistful as he stopped at Pier G and saw *UB-44* lying snugly at her berth. 'You know, sir, I'd give my right arm to be going out on patrol with you today.'

'I know how you feel, Chief, but I'm afraid that's the way the Navy works. Perhaps it's because we younger ones are expendable that they keep you veterans safe on shore.'

'Perhaps,' Herzog agreed gloomily, 'but I know where *I'd* rather be.'

Later that afternoon, fuelled, stored and armed, *UB-44* cast off from the jetty and eased her way out of the crowded harbour. With doubled lookouts, one to cover each quarter of the horizon, the U-boat dug her nose into the sharp swell of the North Sea and set course south-west to take up her routine patrol station on the line of the Haaks lightship southwards to the Broad Fourteens – the historic area where Otto Weddigen and *U-9* had sunk three British cruisers, *Hogue, Aboukir,* and *Cressey,* single-handed on 22 September, 1914. Bergman stared out over the sullen grey waters and wondered whether he would ever achieve a similar fame to Weddigen – Germany's first U-Boat hero. Somehow he thought it unlikely.

The shadows of the afternoon deepened as evening closed in and, just before sunset, Bergman took *UB-44* below the surface for the dangerous twilight period when the eyes played tricks in the fading light. They remained at periscope depth for the next three hours listening to a string of triumphant radio reports of Germany's stunning victories over the Poles which were relayed to the crew over the submarine's loudspeaker system. The men, still excited with the novelty of war, were obviously elated and with every fresh announcement Konrad could see them trying to follow the line of the panzer breakthrough on an old school atlas.

Somehow, the same feeling of elation escaped him. Assuming that the fighting was restricted to Poland the focus of any naval operations must be the Baltic. And yet the majority of the U-boat fleet was scattered across the North Sea and into the Atlantic, hundreds, in some cases thousands, of miles from the scene of action. Perhaps Hitler and his advisers knew something that had not yet been revealed to the German public – that the attack on Poland was certain to bring Britain and France into the conflict. Or perhaps these apparently useless U-boat dispositions were the work of Goering, scheming, as always, to divert the glory of victory from the *Kriegsmarine* to the *Luftwaffe*.

At 2200 hours *UB-44* surfaced to recharge her batteries and, in common with the topsy-turvy life of submarines the world over, Leading Cook Heinrich began preparing the day's main meal in the galley. Cooking was only possible when the U-Boat was running on the surface and, as this was normally during the hours of darkness, dinner was usually served in the small hours after midnight.

Bergman ate his meal in silence with half his mind listening to the martial announcements from Berlin Radio while the other half still puzzled over Doenitz's decision to place the U-Boats – the teeth of the Navy – so far away from the action. And the news that his old ship, the *Pommern*, was in the thick of it and shelling Polish shore positions in support of the advancing Panzers did not help to improve his mood of despondency.

The next day, 2 September, was one of boring routine. Watch diving was not Konrad's favourite form of amusement. And the knowledge that whatever might chance to pass across the lens of his periscope must be allowed to escape scot-free did little to lighten the blackness of his mood. Twice a freighter was sighted and on both occasions *UB-44* slipped beneath the surface to maintain her secretive presence.

It was standard practice for a U-Boat's captain to take the Morning Watch from 4 am to 8 am. Dawn was probably *the* most dangerous time in the entire day and many commanders preferred to take the responsibility on their own shoulders. But all was quiet this morning and Bergman prepared for another fruitless and apparently pointless day's patrol as Hermann Bauer took over at eight bells. The off-duty watch was busy cleaning up the interior of the boat and he stopped for a quick word of encouragement to the men as he walked aft to the wardroom.

Settling back on the leather settee, he thumbed through the night's signals while Brunner, the wardroom steward, brought up a pot of black coffee. The boredom had a soporific effect and the soft hum of the electric motors added a soothing lullaby to his lethargy. His eyelids drooped and he began to doze.

Seven bells had just struck when a new sound stirred the mists of sleep. Bergman was alert and awake within seconds. He listened again. The click of the cypher machine's five unit keyboard in the radio room made him sit up suddenly. There was a sense of urgency in the sounds that brought him to his feet and, pushing aside the wardroom curtains, he went across to the tiny cabinet-sized office opposite. Standing behind the operator he began reading off the signal as it was decoded :

1105-3-9-39. From Naval High Command Stop. To Commanders-in-Chief and Commanders afloat Stop. Great Britain and France have declared war on Germany Stop. Battle stations immediate in accordance with Battle

Instructions for the Navy already promulgated Stop. Raeder.

So Doenitz's dispositions were not quite so ridiculous as he had thought. Operations in the Baltic were of little importance compared with the challenge for the Royal Navy's traditional command of the sea. And now, thanks to the *Kommodore's* foresight, Germany's entire U-Boat fleet was already drawn around the vulnerable lines of sea communication, that were so vital to Britain's existence as a fighting power, like a steel cordon.

Konrad took the microphone of the U-Boat's loudspeaker system in his hand and made a brief announcement of the news to the crew. A spontaneous cheer echoed through the confines of the narrow hull. He pressed the 'speak' button of the microphone again.

'The Fatherland and the safety of our families and homes will depend upon the U-boat service, the *Kriegsmarine,* and our comrades in the *Wehrmacht* and the *Luftwaffe*. I know I can rely on every man in *UB-44* to do his duty.'

The lack of tradition in the *Kriegsmarine* was something Bergman had always regretted and it was in situations such as this that he felt it most. Even so it was ironic that he had to paraphrase the words of his enemy's greatest Admiral to encourage his crew. He hoped that it wasn't an omen for the future.

Franze Mittleburger, *UB-44's* coxswain and the submarine's senior warrant officer, stuck his head into the radio cabin. His eyes looked unnaturally bright with excitement.

'How soon do we hit the bloody English navy, sir?'

'Soon enough, Chief, soon enough. Have you checked the relay valve on No. 5 tank yet? I left a note in the duty log when I came off watch. If it jams up and upsets our trim the next time we dive it could be dangerous.'

'Just going to see about it, sir,' Mittleburger replied cheerfully. 'Had a couple of other little jobs to attend to first.'

He bustled off importantly before Bergman could say anything further.

It was not the first time that Mittleburger had overlooked checking a vital component and Konrad was not over-happy about him. Of course he had an excuse. But then it was a rare occasion when he hadn't. The trouble with the Chief was that he spent too much time reading Nazi propaganda pamphlets and not enough time carrying out his duties efficiently. Being a Party member had given him too many ideas of the wrong sort. Bergman was about to call him back when the cypher machine began chattering again.

'From BDU, sir,' Wolfe said over his shoulder and Konrad leaned forward to read the signal as it came off the decoder.

1116/3/9/39. From Commander-in-Chief U-boats Stop. To Commanding Officers afloat Stop.

Battle Instructions for the U-Boat arm of the Navy are now in force Stop Troopships and merchant ships carrying military equipment to be attacked in accordance with prize regulations of the Hague Convention Stop Enemy convoys to be attacked without warning only on condition that all liners carrying passengers are allowed to proceed in safety Stop These vessels are immune from attack even in convoy Stop Doenitz

So, contrary to popular opinion, they were not going to adopt the policy of *spurlos versenkt** that had brought the U-Boats to the edge of victory in 1917. Bergman's eyebrows lifted in surprise. They were going to play the game by the British rules and fight with one hand virtually tied behind their backs. He opened the safe containing the code books in their specially weighted bags and drew out the buff envelope he had been given shortly before they sailed. Breaking open the seals he pulled out a slip of folded paper with impatient fingers. It was an exciting moment for any officer who still had a streak of romanticism in his blood.

*Sink at sight.

His elation thudded flatly as he scanned the short single sentences.

To Commanding Officer UB-44

You will maintain present patrol line until you have one day's fuel supply left. Return to Wilhelmshaven on completion of patrol. Neutral vessels to be stopped and searched. No action to be taken unless they are carrying contraband goods as listed in OKM List 2, Schedules 4, 5 & 6.

BDU

Bergman put the order back in the safe, turned the key in the lock, and walked across to the bookshelf. He pulled down a large blue-covered volume with buff-coloured loose-leaf pages. Sitting down at the wardroom table he ran through the list of contraband articles in the relevant schedules to refresh his memory. After a few minutes he put the book back in its place and went through into the control room.

'All quiet, sir,' Bauer reported.

Konrad nodded. He conveyed the gist of *UB-44*'s first combat orders and reminded the First Officer to go through the contraband schedules when he went off duty. As he spoke his eyes checked the various dials and gauges clustered in amongst the maze of pipes that festooned every inch of the control-room. They stopped on the gyro repeater, a long strip of thick glass immediately in front of the helmsman's eyes.

'Were you in charge of the off-watch cleaning party, Cox'n?'

'Yes, sir.'

'Why is the gyro repeater still smeared? I remember pointing it out to you before I went down for breakfast.'

Mittleburger leaned over the helmsman's shoulder and peered at the offending instrument.

'Can't understand it, sir. I cleaned that bit of glass myself. Someone must have put their sticky fingers on it.'

He pulled a cloth from his pocket and made a great play of wiping away the smeary marks. The expression on his face made it obvious that he thought the skipper was being petty-minded.

'You're a bloody liar,' thought Bergman. But he said nothing. It was not politic to reprimand a senior warrant officer in front of the ratings without serious cause. But he made a mental note to ball him out privately when they got back to base.

'Down periscope.' Bauer stepped aside as the column sank back into its well. 'Nothing in sight, sir. Not even a fishing boat.'

'They're probably using diversionary routings into Rotterdam,' Bergman told him. 'We'll have to keep moving up and down the line and see if we can locate them. I've got a feeling it's going to be one of *those* patrols with sweet damn-all for our troubles.'

UB-44 spent the rest of the day fruitlessly quartering the Broad Fourteens, searching for the diverted shipping lane but, as Konrad had pessimistically forecast, there was damn all to be seen. The crew had just gone to their stations in readiness for the pre-dusk dive when Baden, the radio room runner, handed the skipper an urgent signal. As Bergman read it, his pessimism vanished.

'Give me a course for Wilhelmshaven, pilot. ETA noon tomorrow.' He turned to Bauer as the navigator bent over the chart table to plot their new track. 'We've had an immediate recall, Number One. Must be something big in the wind. And it's not only us – BDU has called back Kretschmer, Kirchen and a couple of others.'

He turned away to hide the excitement in his face. Perhaps this was the stroke of luck that every U-Boat commander needed if he was to achieve success. Anything was better than this dreary patrolling outside a neutral port. One thing was certain. No matter what Doenitz had in store Bergman knew that *UB-44* would not let him down.

CHAPTER FIVE

The early morning mists were still clearing as the aircraft of 9, 107, 110 and 149 Squadrons lifted into the air from their East Anglian bases, circled once to pick up formation, and then set course for the low-lying islands that skirted the coast of north-west Germany. Although the war was scarcely twenty-four hours old the Royal Air Force was ready to show its teeth to the Nazi tiger in its European lair.

Ten Bristol Blenheim medium bombers and fourteen Vickers Wellington heavy bombers winged their way steadily over the grey calm of the North Sea on the RAF's first strike mission into Germany since November, 1918. And, unlike the sorties that were to follow through the unexpectedly severe winter of 1939-40, they were armed with high-explosive bombs – not harmless propaganda leaflets.

UB-44 was entering Schillig Roads, the vast anchorage that reached down to the landlocked harbour of Wilhelmshaven, when the air raid alarm screamed its first warning. Bergman was on the bridge with Bauer as the wailing sirens drifted faintly across the water and both men assumed it was a practice alarm. But the staccato crack of the warning maroons being fired from the Port War Signal Station soon indicated that this was no drill.

'Anti-aircraft gun crew close up,' Bergman yelled down through the hatch and hurrying feet clattered on the iron ladder as the men clambered to their combat station at the after end of the conning-tower. *Obergefreiter* Werth jammed a slip of 20mm shells into the open maw of the magazine while Nils Boden, the gunlayer, swung the weapon to starboard. All eyes turned towards the seaward horizon searching the blue sky for a glimpse of the enemy.

'Surface lookouts concentrate on your sectors!' Bergman

snapped angrily. 'I don't want to see any man looking upwards – we'll take care of that.'

A group of small black dots shot from the clouds and hurtled down towards the huddled assembly of light grey warships anchored off Brunsbuttel. Tongues of flame sparkled from the cruisers as their guns came into action and a series of dirty grey cottonwool puffs stained the sky. The main formation of bombers made a beeline for the *Emden* and, as they circled away, climbing for altitude across the Roads, *UB-44*'s little gun joined in the fray, pumping 20mm shells at them until its twin barrels were glowing with heat.

Another formation swept in low across the anchorage and two Blenheim bombers peeled off towards the surfaced U-boat. The chatter of their machine-guns seemed unreal and remote until Bergman saw the water splashes of the bullets coming nearer. He felt slightly shocked at the realization that *UB-44* was getting her first taste of war.

'Down!'

Every head ducked behind the thin splinter shield of the conning-tower and there were a series of heavy thuds and whining richochets as the British bullets ripped into the U-boat's steel plating. The 20mm gun hesitated in mid-voice, faltered for a moment and then started to pump shells at the departing aircraft. Konrad hauled himself up from the deck planking. Looking aft he saw a line of bullet holes neatly puncturing the hull plates – the fresh grey paint chipped and gouged to reveal the orange anti-rust coating beneath. Then he realized that the paint was stained with blood which dripped ominously down from the 20mm gun platform.

Werth, the loader, was lying on his back with blood bubbling from his stomach, his hands gripping the steel staunchion in a spasm of pain, Brunner, the wardroom steward, still wearing his white mess jacket, was up beside the gun in Werth's place pushing a fresh clip of shells into the magazine. Boden's cheek was streaked with blood where one of the bullets had grazed his face, but he remained firmly planted in his seat, his hands turning the elevating control wheel as he followed the vanishing aircraft out of range. Petty Officer Essen gave an exuberant thumbs up.

'We got one of the bastards, sir,' he shouted. 'Smack in the port engine. She's down over there.'

Bergman followed the direction of his arm and saw the smoking pyre of the Blenheim on the low line of mud flats that ringed Brunsbuttel.

'Good work!' he shouted back. Then he turned to Bauer. 'Get the loader below, Number One.'

'Two aircraft approaching on starboard bow!'

Bergman looked up to see two more Blenheims skimming the wave tops. There was no time to balance the odds. At this angle the firing arc of the 20mm guns was completely masked by the conning-tower. They were defenceless. And there was always the added chance that their ballast tanks might be punctured in another attack. Bergman acted by instinct and without hesitation. While external damage would not be fatal in home waters it could still entail two or three weeks in drydock for repairs. And the war might be over by then.

'Dive!'

He thumbed the klaxon and, almost simultaneously, heard the water rushing through the Kingston valves into the empty ballast tanks as *UB-44*'s crew carried out the diving routine with practised precision. Bauer slid, almost fell, down the narrow ladder into the control room with Boden and the lookouts following closely behind as the sea lapped over the planking of the foredeck.

The two British aircraft were only four hundred yards away, coming in like a pair of falcons swooping on a frightened rabbit. A wall of water cascaded back over the bridge as the sea smashed against the solid base of the forward deck gun and Bergman, bending over the open

85

hatch, peered through the spray. Where the hell was Essen? Another curtain of water crashed upwards as the sea reached the curved base of the conning-tower and *UB-44* was already running awash in a cauldron of bubbling white foam.

It was like being caught in a heavy downpour of rain. And through the sheets of spray Konrad could see Petty Officer Essen struggling to drag the wounded Werth up the short steel ladder leading from the gun platform. The Blenheims were now only two hundred yards away and the leading aircraft fired a quick burst from his machine-guns to check the range.

'Leave him, Essen!' Bergman shouted. 'Leave him and get below.'

The first bomber roared overhead like an express train. A bomb screeched down, splashed into the sea some fifty yards on the port beam and a great geyser of water erupted as it exploded. It was too far away to cause any damage but the force of the concussion heeled the U-boat sharply to starboard. The second bomber followed moments later and Bergman braced himself for another blast. But nothing happened. The pilot had misjudged the distance and, intent on saving his precious bombs, he put the Blenheim into a steep climb before circling around for a second approach.

Essen reached the hatch opening as the U-boat reeled under the force of the initial bomb blast and Konrad grabbed his shoulders to save him from sliding down into the scuppers. The sea was already flooding in through the drain holes of the conning-tower and there was no time to lose. He bundled the petty officer down through the hatch as the second Blenheim roared in again and, as he dragged the steel cover over his head, Bergman saw Werth's body rolling limply like a rag-doll. The staring terror on the loader's face imprinted itself into his mind as he fastened the dog-catches and abandoned the wounded man to his fate.

'Thirty feet, sir. Motors grouped up – full ahead. Trim

level,' Bauer reported as Bergman entered the brightly lit control room.

Bergman nodded. Water was streaming off his sodden uniform and, stripping off the jacket, he threw it on the floor.

'Up periscope.'

Gripping the handles he swung the lens towards the bows and searched the sky. He saw the two Blenheims bank to the right, their red, white and blue markings gleaming in the sun, as they returned to the attack.

'How much depth, pilot?'

'Fifty feet but shoaling, sir,' Hauptmann reported. 'No rocks and the bottom's only mud.'

'Fifty feet, Number One!'

'Fifty feet, sir.'

The hydroplanes tilted and *UB-44*'s bows angled down as the motors drove her deeper. Bauer was just catching trim when the concussion of an exploding bomb just below the surface made the U-boat shudder from stem to stern.

'Thank God they're not using depth-charges, Number One,' Bergman said quietly. 'They'll have to get a direct hit to do any damage with ordinary HE bombs – and at this depth the fuzes will detonate long before they get anywhere near. Let's go up and see what's happening.'

Bauer ordered *UB-44* to thirty feet and Bergman waited as the periscope slid from its well. He took a quick 360° sweep of the sky.

'Well *they* won't bother us any more,' he observed with satisfaction. 'A couple of Me 109s are chasing them out to sea.' He looked through the eyepiece intently and every man in the control room waited expectantly. The skipper was their only contact with the world above the surface and Bergman, having experienced a similar feeling of remoteness when he had been serving as a subordinate officer, knew the psychological value of keeping them in touch with a running commentary.

'The second bomber is trailing smoke from its port engine . . . it's trying to climb. There's a 109 right on its tail . . . he's tearing it to pieces with his cannon . . . the crew are baling out and its coming down . . . it's gone into the sea about two miles to the east.'

There was a cheer from the crew as they heard the vivid commentary over the internal loudspeakers and Bergman was pleased to see that their moral was still high despite the surprised shock of the first attack.

'Take a look, Number One,' he said, as he stepped back from the periscope.

Bauer continued the commentary while Konrad moved slowly around the control room checking the dials and instruments. Some instinct warned him that not every man was concentrating on his job. Glancing up at the inclometer he saw that the bows of the U-boat were lifting slightly and then falling back like a mechanical see-saw. He turned sharply and saw Mittleburger, the coxswain and the man responsible for controlling the diving-planes, deep in conversation with Essen, the Petty Officer in charge of the AA gun. It was obvious that Mittleburger was agitated about something and that Essen was doing his best to calm him. Bergman sensed trouble.

'Stand down, Cox'n,' he said crisply. 'Schwartz, take over the hydroplane controls – and damp down that oscillating motion.' He turned to Bauer. 'What's the situation topsides, Number One?'

'All over, sir. The Port War Signal Station is flying the "All Clear" and *Emden* seems to have ceased fire.'

'Right – take her up. Put a double sky-watch on as soon as we surface. And ask PWSS for berthing instructions – the raid may have changed our previous orders.'

'Stand by to surface. Blow all tanks.'

While Bauer took *UB-44*'s crew through the old familiar routine Bergman returned to the Coxswain who was still standing by the hydroplane control panel with an aggrieved look on his face.

'I'll see you in my cabin.'

The captain's cabin was a six feet square area at one end of the wardroom and it was created by the simple expedient of pulling two dark green curtains across. Mittleburger stood to attention as Bergman closed the heavy drapes. He looked sullen and there was an expression in his eyes that warned of danger.

Bergman sat down in front of his tiny desk. 'You have been guilty of various breaches of discipline recently, Mittleburger, but I have tried to make allowances for you by putting it down to the strains of uncertainty we have all endured these last few weeks. There can, however, be no excuse for mishandling the boat when we are in action. I intend to put in a disciplinary report when we get back to base and, in the meantime, you are relieved from duty. Have you anything to say?'

'You left Werth up there to drown.'

There was no mistaking the venom in the man's voice but Bergman chose to ignore it. He treated it as a rational question rather than an accusation.

'I had no choice, Mittleburger. Werth was dying – he may have already been dead – and I cannot hazard the safety of the boat for one man whether he is dead or alive. Five more seconds on the surface and that last stick of bombs would have hit us. I realize it is hard to sacrifice a comrade but in war these things happen. There may well come a day when I have to sacrifice *UB-44*, myself and every man in the crew for the sake of saving the Fatherland.

Mittleburger was still standing to attention but his hands were trembling with rage.

'Murderer!'

'Take a grip on yourself, man! Think what you are saying.'

The Coxswain's face was red with anger as he faced Berg-

89

man across the tiny cabin. Suddenly he collapsed, tears streaming down his face.

'Murderer – bloody murderer,' he sobbed.

Konrad pushed the red 'alert' button on the left-hand side of his writing desk. Almost immediately Essen, *UB-44*'s Master-at-Arms, accompanied by one of the seamen, pushed through the curtains and entered the cabin.

'Warrant Officer Mittleburger is to be placed under close arrest,' Bergman told him. 'He is to be handed over to the Shore Police as soon as we berth.' He looked at the sobbing man and felt suddenly sorry for him. 'And see if you can find some sort of sedative for him in the medicine cabinet.'

Bergman shut the curtains to restore his privacy and, sitting down at the desk, he rested his chin in his cupped hands. For the first time since *UB-44* had crash-dived to escape the bombers the chilling reality of what he had done hit him.

Mittleburger was right. He *had* murdered one of his own men. So much for the romantic dreams of becoming a U-boat hero, sinking a record-breaking tonnage of enemy shipping and winning honour and glory in the heat of battle. All he had to show for his first action was a damaged boat and a dead man.

The truth was harsh and unpalatable. Instead of fighting it out like a man he had scuttled for safety under the surface at the first opportunity. And he had deliberately sacrificed one of his men – a man who had been wounded doing his duty in the face of the enemy – to save his own skin. And when his senior NCO had dared to tell him the truth he had put the man under arrest.

Bergman raised his head and crushed his clasped fingers together – the physical action mirroring the inner mental struggle he was enduring.

The news of Mittleburger's arrest quickly reached the crew and the men on duty in the control room were uncomfortably silent as Bergman ducked through the bulkhead door. Was it imagination or were they deliberately concentrating on their instruments to avoid meeting his eyes? He reached the bottom of the conning-tower steps and hauled himself up to the bridge. *UB-44* was snugly berthed against the pier and Bauer had just dismissed the mooring party. He saluted.

'All secure, sir. What are your orders?'

Konrad forced the self-doubts from his mind and tried to adjust to the less demanding routine of day-to-day problems.

'Report the damage to the Dockyard Superintendent. And tell him I want *U-44* back and ready for service within twelve hours.'

'Any leave or late passes, sir?'

'No. The duty watch is to check all stores and load replacement supplies as necessary. The off-duty watch can clean up. Anything else?'

Bauer hesitated. 'A couple of the older men asked to see the Padre about a short memorial service for Werth. Can you give permission?'

'No, Herr Leutnant. Seaman Werth died doing his duty for the Fatherland. In my view *that* is sufficient memorial in itself. And now, if there is nothing else, I must make my report to the Flotilla Commander.'

He found Petty Officer Essen waiting for him at the end of the gangway. As Bergman appeared he snapped smartly to attention and saluted.

'May I speak to you for a moment, sir?'

'Of course, Essen. What's the trouble?'

'No trouble, sir. I just wanted to say, on behalf of the men, that they don't hold the same opinions as the Cox'n. Begging your pardon, sir, but they all thought you did the right thing.'

Bergman felt at a loss for words. While still assailed by his own self-doubts it was, at least, a relief to know that he retained the confidence of his men.

'Thank you, Essen. But, tell me, why the silence in the boat just now – and all this nonsense about a memorial service?'

'Well, sir, they felt a bit embarrassed over what the Cox'n is supposed to have said. They thought you might think they felt the same. As to this memorial service, well, I must admit that I'm as puzzled about that as you are, sir. I've never known this bunch of heathens to go rushing to the padre before.'

Bergman turned to go down the gangplank.

'I won't have the padre messing about on *my* boat, Essen. But you can tell the men that, if they wish it, I will hold a brief service myself next time we go out on patrol.' He grinned suddenly. 'And for your private information, Petty Officer, I haven't overlooked the fact that there's a wet canteen right next door to the Padre's office and I've forbic'den all shore leave. I think there might be some connection to the crew's sudden religious mania.'

Headquarters of the 10th Flotilla was only a few yards from the end of Pier G but by the time Bergman reached the sand-bagged entrance he was beginning to recover his sense of proportion.

Kapitan Walther, Commanding Officer of the 10th Flotilla, listened to his report impassively. He asked several searching questions about the air attack and the decision to dive – questions that gave Konrad an uneasy feeling. But he answered each one as truthfully as he could and made no attempt to evade the responsibility of his decision. Walther's face was a mask and it was impossible to judge his reactions. When he had finished listening to the report the Flotilla Leader sat staring out of the window without speaking for a full half minute. Then, swinging his chair around sharply, he gestured for Bergman to sit down.

'In my judgement your actions were perfectly in order, Herr Oberleutnant,' he said quietly. 'It is never pleasant to sacrifice a man, especially a wounded man, to save one's ship. But in the circumstances I consider you had no alternative. As for Mittleburger he is clearly in need of psychiatric treatment. I will have him transferred out of *UB-44* immediately. No court martial or disciplinary enquiry, you understand; it would not be good for morale.'

Kapitan Walther leaned back in his chair and began tapping the top of the desk with his index finger.

'The problem is going to be finding a replacement. Experienced Warrant Officers are like gold these days. Either they're already assigned or else they're on instructional duties. Do you have any suggestion, *Herr Oberleutnant*?'

Bergman's mind was equally blank. As a relative newcomer to the U-boat branch he knew very few Warrant Officers and, following Walther's example, he too stared out of the window for inspiration. As he looked down he suddenly saw a small grey Opel Kadet sweep around the corner of the Torpedo Stores and stop outside the main Headquarter's building.

'Any objection to an over-age man, *Herr Kapitan*?'

Walther shook his head. 'In the present circumstances – none. Providing the man's not *too* old.'

'How about Herzog, sir? He's driving a staff car for BDU and he's only about two years over the limit.'

'Yes, I know the man you mean,' Walther nodded. 'An excellent record and still as fit as a fiddle. But does *he* want to go back on combat operations at his age?'

Bergman smiled.

'Just tell him I want him on board *UB-44* by midnight, sir. I think the expression on his face will answer your question.'

An hour later, having finished his solitary lunch in the dining-room of the Officers' Mess, Konrad made his way up the sweeping marble stairs to the *Kommando* Room – a room reserved solely for the use of off-duty U-boat commanders where they could relax and discuss 'shop' without the embarrassment of being overheard by subordinates. It was a useful and practical abode and in its creation Doenitz had shown, yet again, that he understood the needs of the men who had to endure the stresses and strains of combat command under the sea. Rank and seniority did not exist behind the doors of the *Kommando* Room. That every man inside was a U-boat captain was sufficient.

By the time Bergman arrived the other commanders who had been recalled with *UB-44* were already comfortably ensconced in deep leather armchairs discussing the rumours that were circulating around the U-boat base. He recognized Otto Kretschmer, whom he had not seen since his first introductory trip in a submarine some three years earlier, Endrass, Liebing, Gunther Prien, and the familiar smiling face of Kirchen.

'Well, how do you like this?' Hans asked, as Bergman dropped into a chair beside him. 'The second day of the war and here we are sitting on our backsides ashore.'

Konrad grunted. He was sure they had been recalled ready for some major operation. And, in any case, after his first taste of action in the Schillig Roads that morning he felt entitled to a few brief hours of respite ashore.

'Have you heard about Churchill and the *Athenia*?' Hans asked.

Konrad shook his head. 'No – what's happened? And what's the *Athenia* anyway?'

'She's a passenger liner on the New York run. She sank this morning and the British are saying a U-boat put a torpedo into her last night. You know, all the usual atrocity stuff.'

'But we've got orders not to sink passenger ships without warning – you must have got it wrong, Hans.'

'No I haven't. And that's the point, old boy. Berlin radio is claiming that Churchill ordered a Royal Navy submarine to sink her so they could blame it on us. And I wouldn't put it past them. Trouble is that the Yanks will believe anything the British tell them.'*

'It's not a very good start, I suppose,' said Konrad. 'But I don't see how it will affect our U-boat operations.'

'Well, I'll tell you how,' Kirchen told him. 'BDU has already issued additional instructions informing us not to sink passenger ships unless they are in convoy. It's just like last time. The British have got us beaten before we've fired a single shot. We're the Hun baby-killers again just as we were in 1917. It makes me bloody sick. You know that bastard Churchill would turn the Royal Navy's guns on the French fleet if he thought it would win the war for him.†

Kapitanleutnant Liebling broke in to change the subject. 'I hear you were caught in the raid this morning, Bergman. Any damage or casualties?'

'I lost one of my gunners but the boat's not too bad. Only a few bullet holes where they don't really matter. We were lucky, I guess.'

'It was more than luck,' said Kretschmer. 'I was watching the affair through my glasses. If you had not dived when you did that last stick of bombs would have plastered you.'

'Thanks – I only wish I could feel as sure,' Bergman said

*The Donaldson liner *Athenia* (13,581 tons) was torpedoed by Kapitanleutnant Lemp's *U-30* on the night of 3 September, 1939. She sank the following day in position 56°44′N – 14°05′W with the loss of 112 lives including a number of American nationals. Doenitz was unaware that a U-boat was responsible for the attack until Lemp returned to base almost a week later. In the interval, and relying on Doenitz's denials that a U-boat was responsible, Dr Goebbels Propaganda Ministry concocted a story that the *Athenia* had been sunk on Churchill's instructions in order to blame the Germans. Lemp's excuse for the attack was that he had mistaken the liner for an auxiliary cruiser.

†Kirchen's words were sadly prophetic. In 1940, after France had surrendered, Churchill sent the British Navy to Oran and ordered it to open fire on the French warships anchored there to prevent them from falling into the hands of the Germans. 1,297 French sailors were killed by the guns of their former Allies.

ruefully. 'I keep thinking I should have stayed on the surface and fought it out.'

'Nonsense. They caught you on your blind spot.' Kretschmer drew a quick sketch on his newspaper. 'Coming in over the bows was quite a bright idea – your AA gun was completely masked by the conning-tower. Your only alternative to diving would have been to swing broadside on and give your gunners a chance. But look at the target you would have presented to the bombers if you had. No, take it from me, you were absolutely right to dive. In those circumstances I would have done exactly the same.'

It was a relief to hear an experienced U-boat captain like Kretschmer confirming the action he had taken. Professionally speaking he realized that he had done the right thing despite his initial doubts. But Bergman could still see the frozen terror on Werth's face when he realized that *UB-44* was submerging and leaving him to drown. *That* was something he would take a long time to forget.

There was a sharp click from the Telefunken loudspeaker high up on the wall as the public address system was switched through.

'*Achtung*! *Achtung*! *Kapitanleutnant* Prien and *Oberleutnant* Bergman to report to Flotilla Commander immediately.'

'Lucky you,' said Hans as Konrad stood up. 'You go off to honour and glory while I sit around polishing my arse on a leather armchair. Well, I'm for another drink.' He turned to Kretschmer and the other captains. 'How about you?'

They shook their heads politely. Their own names might be called at any minute, and they wanted cold clear heads when they were.

Kapitan Heinrich Walther was pacing his narrow office when Prien and Bergman reported. He wasted no time on preliminaries.

'You presumably know already about the *Athenia* incident,' he began. The two men nodded. 'As yet we don't know what the true facts behind the sinking are but BDU intends to take no chances and a General Order is being issued reminding all commanders afloat of the restrictions imposed by International Law and, in addition, forbidding attacks on any passenger ship sailing unescorted. There have been high level discussions with OKM by telephone and it has been decided to divert the U-boat offensive away from merchant shipping for the time being and concentrate our attacks on enemy warships.'

Walther paused for a few moments as if gathering his thoughts. 'You may, of course, still attack a merchant ship but only on condition that you first surface, examine her papers for contraband, and give her crew sufficient time to get away in the ship's boats.'

Why bother to use submarines at all, Bergman thought to himself. It was the 1915 situation all over again. Put yourself at a tactical disadvantage but make sure the enemy has all the aces. Everyone knew that Britain was arming her merchant ships and any U-boat commander surfacing near one of them was virtually inviting his own suicide. Still, if these were the orders it was his duty to obey them no matter how stupid they appeared to be. He glanced at Prien but the Kapitanleutnant's bland expressionless face gave no hint of his inner feelings.

'Your two boats, *U-47* and *UB-44*, have been selected for our first strike against the Royal Navy,' Walther continued. 'Your target, gentlemen, will be Scapa Flow – the Home Fleet's main anchorage.' He walked across to the wall charts and pulled down a detailed large-scale map of the target area. Bergman was listening but his mind was in a whirl. The whole idea seemed preposterously impossible. No one had ever succeeded in penetrating the Flow's deadly defences before. Two had tried it – von Hennig in *U-18* was ambushed and sunk by patrol vessels on 23 November, 1914, and had been lucky to escape with his life; and Kapitanleutnant Emsmann, making a do-or-die attack on the base on 28 October, 1918, with *UB-116,* had been killed in a controlled minefield. And now he and Prien were to be given the same dice-loaded chance of death or glory. Trying to shrug off the queasy feeling in his stomach he leaned forward attentively as the Flotilla Chief briefed them on the latest intelligence information concerning Scapa Flow's formidable defences.

Dusk was closing its velvet shroud over the dockyard as the two officers walked past the lengthening shadows of the barrack blocks towards the harbour. They stopped at the entrance to Pier G and shook hands in silence. Then, while Bergman checked his identity with the guard, Prien trudged on down the stone jetty to *U-47*.

It was a cool night and the mists were already rising gently from the sluggish waters of the harbour basin. Konrad shivered and wished he had brought his greatcoat with him as he made his way along the narrow pier. For the first time he was struck by the stringent black-out regulations and the darkness seemed to add to the chill of the night air. He missed the comforting glow of *UB-44*'s lights beckoning him home and he swore quietly to himself as he tripped over an unseen bollard.

The end of the gangway loomed into vision and, reaching for the handrail, he groped his way down to the deck. Heavy blankets screened the inside of the conning-tower hatch and Bergman pushed through them, pulled up the lower hatch and dropped down into the cosy warmth of the well-lit control room. It was almost like coming home to a blazing log-fire after a night's hunting on the Grunenburg.

His new coxswain was waiting at the foot of the ladder – his battered face wreathed in a broad smile of greeting. He saluted smartly.

'*Oberbootsmann* Herzog reporting for duty, sir. And thank you for mentioning my name to the *Kapitan*, sir.'

Bergman nodded. Herzog's obvious delight at being posted back to an operational U-boat boded well for the future and he had no doubts about the veteran's efficiency. A stiffening of experienced older men was just what *UB-44*'s crew needed and, backed up by Essen, he felt sure that the coxswain's example would soon be reflected in every aspect of the boat's life and work. He slipped off his coat.

'We are sailing at midnight, Chief. Are we fully kitted up?'

'Yes, sir. The Flotilla Torpedo officer insisted we unloaded our normal outfit for routine servicing and testing. We've shipped *G7e Mk III's* as replacements.'

Bergman raised his eyebrows. So they were getting the new electric torpedoes. BDU must rate him pretty highly to entrust him with what were virtually secret weapons.

'Good – and are all provisions on board?'

'Yes, sir. The off-duty watch are packing them away at the moment. We should be finished and cleaned up by 2300 hours.'

'Carry on, Cox'n.' Bergman turned to Bauer, Hauptmann, the navigating officer, and Veitch, the engineer officer. 'Will you come along to the wardroom please, gentlemen.'

Bauer pulled the curtains together as they sat around the narrow table.

'Repairs completed, Number One?'

'Yes, sir. The Superintendent said it was only superficial damage and the shipwrights have patched the holes with plates. We refuelled while you were at Flotilla HQ.'

'How about the Met report, pilot?'

Hauptmann consulted his notebook. 'There's a trough of low pressure in the middle of the North Sea around Dogger and there's another low coming in over the Shetlands. If we're heading westwards I'd say it's likely to be bloody rough.'

Bergman smiled. He was under orders not to reveal their destination until they were at sea – a routine precaution for nearly all operations. So Hauptmann could not possibly know their probable direction.

But he was certainly right about one thing. It was going to be bloody rough in *all* senses of the word.

CHAPTER SIX

The gales forecast by Hauptmann finally blew themselves out by mid-afternoon and the heavy seas subsided to a sullen swell that made *UB-44* roll with stomach-churning violence. It was bad enough for the men exposed to the elements on the open bridge of the submarine but it was a thousand times worse for those cooped up inside the iron hull. More than a dozen were already prostrate with sea-sickness and the airless atmosphere of the U-boat smelled sourly of diesel oil, stale cabbage water, human sweat and vomit.

Most of the stores so carefully housed and husbanded by Herzog before they left Wilhelmshaven were now scattered wildly over the floor, sliding and slithering in the revolting mess that swirled like an uncooked omelette at every heavy lurch of the unhappy U-boat. And Herzog, incredibly enjoying the challenge, chivvied the off-duty watch into clearing up the shambles.

Hauptmann suffered the agony of sea-sickness more than anyone and he kept an iron bucket alongside his table as he crouched forward plotting the course on the charts. The clammy dampness of his hands smudged the paper while the urgent demands of nature made him break off from his calculations every few minutes and bend helplessly over the bucket.

UB-44 continued pushing northwards towards Scapa, her narrow bows digging deeply into the heavy seas and throwing a wall of spray back over the men on the bridge. The temperature had fallen sharply and the drops of water stung like hard chips of ice. But, despite their discomfort, never for a moment did they relax their vigilance. And, as dusk deepened into night, the seas mercifully calmed and the wind faded to a light breeze. Overhead the grey storm clouds that had scudded across the sky throughout the day slowed to a gentle amble and finally cleared to reveal the vast blackness of the night sky with its canopy of twinkling stars.

Bergman was feeling optimistic when he came off watch at midnight. They would be within visual distance of the Flow by dawn and the rapidly improving weather conditions boded well for their task – an unexpected stroke of good fortune after the storm they had endured throughout the day. He confided his thoughts to Herzog who was still in the control room cleaning up the mess.

'I wouldn't be too sure about that, sir,' he said dismally when Bergman had finished. 'There's only two types of weather in these latitudes – gales or fogs. Now that the wind's dropped I'll lay ten marks to a pfennig we'll be running in thick fog within three hours.'

'Don't be such a bloody jonah, Chief. The weather is improving every hour. By dawn we'll be able to take visual bearings and pin-point our exact position before we dive. It'll be child's play.'

But for all of Konrad's optimism Herzog's mournful prophecy proved correct and when he came up to take over the Morning Watch at 0400 hours he found *UB-44* crawling on the surface in a flat calm completely shrouded in a blanket of thick fog. Not even the bows were visible from the bridge, and the jumping wire, dripping with beads of moisture, disappeared into the swirling mist as it angled down towards the net cutters at the stem.

'Visibility is about twenty yards, sir,' Bauer reported, as the skipper joined him in the conning-tower, 'and it's been closing in like this ever since midnight.'

Bergman stared out into the damply swirling fog and cursed quietly to himself. Unless they could obtain visual bearings any attempt to penetrate the Flow was doomed to failure.

'I wonder how Prien's getting on, sir,' Bauer mused.

'Bogged down the same as us, I imagine. He should be

standing to the north by dawn. Walther wanted him to wriggle inside the defences through the Kirk Channel although it means he will have to contend with a very strong tide race. Our route's through the Holm Channel to the east. But Christ knows where we are in this muck!'

'I got a star sight just after midnight, sir. It means we have one firm fix if nothing else. Hauptmann's plotting our position by dead reckoning.'

Bergman stood in silent thought for a few moments. His coat was running with water where the damp foggy air had settled on the leather and he shivered as the clammy chill penetrated his clothing. No wonder rheumatism is an occupational disease of U-boat commanders, he thought. Leaving Bauer on Watch he turned and went down the ladder into the bright warmth of the control room.

Hauptmann was working on his charts – his face still pale from the rigours of the storm, although Herzog had had the forethought to remove the offending bucket. Bergman leaned across the table and studied the carefully traced pencil lines. He pointed to one of the marks.

'Is this Bauer's astro fix?'

'Yes, sir. Time reported as 0023 hours. I've been following every course change since then. There's no wind to speak of but I've had to make some estimated corrections for the tide.' He glanced up at the Leitz chronometer, checked off a distance on his dividers and jabbed it into the chart. 'We're just about *here* at the moment.'

Bergman looked. The position indicated by the pointed tip of the dividers was less than three miles from the rocky coast of Rose Ness. Certainly too close for comfort in this fog. The conly consolation lay in the fact that they were probably in 30 fathoms of water which meant plenty of room to dive deep in an emergency.

'How accurate is "just about", Pilot?'

Hauptmann considered the question for a few moment. Then he shrugged. 'The tides are a bit unpredictable –

especially after last night's gale. I'd say give or take two miles.'

Bergman studied the chart again. Two miles eastwards would be safe enough. But two miles westwards would place them inside the Inner Patrol line and in shoaling water as shallow as 24 feet – less than periscope depth. No joy there. And the position was even worse if they were at a tangent to their estimated track. Northwest would put *UB-44* in imminent danger of running ashore on the rocky crags of the mainland where treacherous shallows skirted the cliffs – while to the southwest were the double dangers of Burray Ness and the shoals, some less than 6 feet, in the entrance to Water Sound.

The prize might be great but, to Bergman's mind, the dangers were even greater. There was no point in hazarding the U-boat when the target would not even be visible through the periscope. Survival, that primeval instinct that had guided his judgement in the Schillig Roads, now dominated his mind. He stood back from the chart table and turned to the helmsman.

'Reverse course, *steurmann*. Steer on reciprocal bearing.'

The steel-spoked wheel spun as Dichter obeyed the order and Hauptmann made a routine note of the course change on his charts. As Bergman crossed to the bridge ladder he saw Herzog's head move in an almost imperceptible nod. Then he climbed up through the lower hatch to the deck.

The fog was still as thick as ever and the throb of the diesels boomed back as the sound echoed in the clammy stillness.

'We're running away, Bauer,' he said shortly.

Bauer smiled wryly. 'I'd scarcely call four knots *running*, sir. And in any case there's not much point trying to force Holm Sound when we don't even know where it is.'

He's a good officer, Bergman thought to himself. But he's only saying it to keep me happy. He stared moodily into the fog. He was beginning to doubt whether he really had the

103

right qualities for a U-boat command. First there was Werth – and now this. On both occasions he had chosen to escape rather than face up to danger. Was it only extreme caution and a mature understanding of the responsibilities that lay in the loneliness of command? Or was it sheer cowardice? The agony of not knowing his own inner motives made the decision even more difficult to accept.

'Is there a bow lookout, Number One?' The question had to be asked as it was impossible to see forward as far as the stem.

'Yes, sir. I put Schoen up there when I came on Watch. He's got the best pair of eyes and ears on the boat.'

'Right, get him back here and then clear the bridge. We're going to dive but I don't want to sound the klaxon in case there's a British patrol nearby. Get below and tell them in the control room. You may begin flooding as soon as I'm through the lower hatch.'

Schoen, his hands blue with cold and his eyes red-rimmed with strain, clambered up to the bridge and followed the other members of duty watch down the ladder. Bauer brought up the rear and Bergman waited until he heard the diesels die away. Then he, too, slid through the hatch and joined them in the control room below.

'Echo sounder?'

'Thirty fathoms, sir.'

'Right, take her to 100 feet, Cox'n.' He turned to Bauer. 'All hands can stand down, Number One. We're likely to be at diving stations for a long time if this fog persists.'

Bergman's prediction proved uncomfortably accurate.

1800 hours. 6-9-39. Remained submerged all day. Visibility almost nil. Sea conditions calm. No wind. No HE or visual contacts.

0200 hours. 7-9-39. Surfaced to recharge batteries. Thick fog persists. Course 150 at half speed. Hands to dinner. Sea conditions calm. No wind.

2200 hours. 8-9-39. Fog lifted slightly. Surfaced for astro-

fix. Position now established. Variation twelve miles north-east of DR position. Sea remains calm. Wind increased to Force 2. Nothing sighted for three days.

He slipped the pencil back into his pocket after initialling the last entry in the deck log and walked slowly round the control room inspecting the instruments before going through to the wardroom. Bauer was sitting moodily at the table playing *Doppelkopf** with *UB-44*'s engineering officer. Bergman poured himself some coffee and joined them.

'I've decided to leave the area if we're still fogbound when we surface at midnight. My alternative orders permit a normal patrol if it proves impossible to carry out our main mission. Perhaps we'll have more luck hunting merchant ships.'

'We could hardly have less,' Bauer said pointedly. 'It was a damn fool idea sending us into the Flow anyway – it was a 100 to 1 that we'd ever get out again.'

Bergman shrugged. 'Perhaps, but we had to obey orders. I know one thing though. The fog might have bitched *us* but I'll bet Prien got *U-47* into Scapa despite the weather.'

As it happened his guess was wrong. Pinned down by the fog, Prien had circled off the Kirk Channel for less than 24 hours and then, with less patience than Bergman, he turned east in search of fairer game. Initially his luck was out but on the 5th, while *UB-44* was still lying sub-merged off Scapa Flow waiting for the fog to lift, *U-47* halted a British steamer, the *Bosnia,* and sent her to the bottom with a torpedo.

Bergman, too, found better luck once he was clear of the hoodoo-haunted waters of the Orkneys. After spending three fruitless days astride the trade route linking Britain with the Norwegian port of Bergen an unknown ship was finally sighted on the northern horizon during the forenoon watch. *UB-44* was running on the surface but, in obedience

*A card game popular with U-boat crews. In the Royal Navy submariners preferred 'uckers' – a variation of Ludo.

to operational orders, he took the U-boat down and inspected his potential victim through the periscope as she steamed closer.

'Seems harmless enough,' he told Bauer. 'No sign of any guns and she's deep laden with freight – probably iron ore. And she's not flying any flag so she could well be British. Stand by to surface. We'll try firing a warning shot.'

Bauer passed the routine orders down the boat and the gun crew closed up at the bottom of the ladder ready to rush on deck as soon as the conning-tower pushed up above the surface. The signalman waited behind them clasping his portable 6-inch lamp. Just aft, in the magazine, the shells were being stacked ready for immediate use, and every man on board felt the tension tingling in his blood as the final moments ticked by.

'Surface!'

UB-44 rushed upwards, the compressed air hissing as the water was blown through the valves of her ballast tanks. A cauldron of white foam frothed above her and then, streaming water, her conning-tower broke surface on the freighter's port quarter. Bergman had already unclipped the lower hatch and he threw the heavy counter-balanced lid up with a quick thrust of his arm. Then, followed by the gun's crew, the signaller and the four lookouts, he climbed agilely up the ladder, unfastened the upper hatch and emerged into the fresh clean-tasting air.

'Fire one shot across the bows, Essen!'

The 3.5-inch quick-firer swung to starboard and a shell slid into the breech. Mucken slammed the breech-block shut and pushed down the locking lever.

The shell exploded in a geyser of dirty brown water some fifty yards in front of the freighter's bows. As the next round was being rammed home Bergman turned to the signaller.

'Tell her to stop.'

Zerman's finger flashed the letter 'K' at ten second

intervals.* Bergman saw the bow wave of the merchant ship fall away as she obeyed.

'Cease fire!'

He moved across to the voicepipe linking the bridge to the wireless cabin.

'Are they using their radio, Wolfe?'

'Yes, sir. They're transmitting a continuous repetition signal *"SS Haven Court being attacked by U-Boat"*.'

'Is there any position being given?'

'No, sir. They seem to have overlooked that in their panic.'

'That's a relief,' thought Bergman. It meant that *UB-44* was in no immediate danger of a counter-attack. Without an accurate position it would be like searching for a needle in a haystack. Even so, the radio warning made him angry, and it demonstrated the futility of BDU's orders to surface and challenge before attacking. He leaned forward over the edge of the conning-tower.

'Silence their radio, Essen!'

UB-44's second shot struck the steamer's bridge with a searing yellow flash. Splintered wood and torn metal flew in all directions. The third shell demolished a small white cabin just abaft the chartroom at the rear of the bridge.

'Radio has ceased transmission,' Wolfe reported laconically.

'I'm not surprised,' thought Bergman. He ordered the U-Boat to hold fire. The insistent phrasing of the Geneva Convention kept revolving in his brain – the safety of the crew must be ensured. There must be no more firing until *Haven Court's* men were safely clear of the ship.

'The enemy is abandoning ship, sir.'

Bergman raised his glasses to confirm the lookout's report. It was the first time he had seen a ship being abandoned and he found it an unnerving sight. *Haven Court's* boats were being lowered with desperate speed and it was obvious

*In the International Code the letter 'K' means: *You should stop your vessel immediately.*

that they expected the U-boat to open fire again. The Port-1 lifeboat was engulfed in flames from the fires started by *UB-44*'s shells and another boat tipped over on striking the water throwing its occupants into the icy sea. But two more of the ship's boats safely cleared the side of the abandoned freighter and began moving east under oars after stopping to drag their comrades from the water. Bergman studied them carefully through his binoculars. Many of the crew had obviously been in their bunks when the U-boat appeared and most were wearing little more than underwear or pyjamas. The air was chill, with a hint of frost, and the Norwegian coast was a good eighty miles to the east. He felt a sudden sympathy for them.

The last boat, a motor dory, was still swinging gently against the side of the steamer and Bergman frowned as he saw a woman being carefully helped into it. An icy hand clutched his heart. He picked up his glasses and looked again but there was no mistake. Surely he hadn't attacked a passenger ship. That really would be the last straw after BDU's firm edict on the subject.

'Bauer! Check the list for the SS *Haven Court*. Hurry!'

The engine of the motor dory coughed to life and the little boat swung away from the steamer in a wide circle and headed in the opposite direction to the other two lifeboats.

'Clutches in! Full ahead both. Steer to intercept.'

UB-44 belched greasy smoke from her exhausts as she set off in pursuit. With her powerful 2,800 hp MAN diesels she could outrun the tiny motor boat with ease and, as if realizing the unequal struggle, the dory suddenly slowed and turned towards the submarine.

'Stop engines. Bring her round so that she comes in alongside our lee, Herzog.'

The U-boat slowed gently and turned protectively as the motor-boat nosed towards her port beam where the hull provided some protection from the wind. Bergman waited until her bows were bumping *UB-44*'s ballast tanks and picked up a megaphone.

'Will the Captain please acknowledge?' he shouted in English.

A tall figure stood up in the stern – his gold brimmed cap contrasting strangely with the blue striped pyjamas he was wearing. He saluted in reply to Bergman's request.

'Ship's name, destination, and cargo?'

'*Haven Court* for Newcastle carrying iron ore.'

Bauer thrust a copy of Lloyd's Register towards Konrad and pointed his finger half-way down the opened page. Bergman glanced down. Just an ordinary freighter – well, that was a relief. But how the hell did the woman come into it?

The two vessels, one grimly efficient in its grey paint, the other overcrowded and pathetically inadequate, had now drifted so closely together that two of *UB-44*'s seamen had to stand on the foredeck casing fending them apart with boathooks like herdsmen gently separating two sheep.

'Do you have a compass, Captain?'

The Englishman nodded.

'Steer 0-8-5. Landfall should be about eighty miles and the weather forecast is good. Is there anything you need?'

'We could do with some clothes or some blankets.' He gestured towards the huddled group sitting in the stern. 'Two of the men were injured by the shell-fire and my wife needs something to keep her warm.'

Bergman saw the woman sitting beside her husband. She was young, dark haired and attractive. But her face and arms were already blue from exposure. She had been asleep in her cabin when *UB-44* had opened fire and Konrad could see her nipples standing stiffly erect with cold under her flimsy nightgown. He looked away with embarrassment.

'Bauer! Send up some coats and blankets. And get a couple of our emergency first-aid kits and some Schnapps – take some of mine from the wardroom cabinet.'

Clambering down on to the slippery fore-deck casing he dragged off his thick leather topcoat and handed it to the woman. She took it gratefully, slipped her arms into the still-warm sleeves, and snuggled down inside it. Essen contributed his white woollen muffler while *UB-44*'s gunlayer, determined not to be outdone, slipped off his heavy sea boots and passed them into the dory for the woman to put on.

'Thank you, *Herr Oberleutnant*,' Captain Wilkinson said quietly, 'I appreciate your kindness. I am glad to see that the German Navy has not forgotten the meaning of chivalry. If you will tell me your boat's number I will make sure that the Admiralty is informed of your conduct.'

'I am sorry, Captain, but I cannot reveal our identity. I only hope my men will receive similar treatment when our turn comes – which I'm sure it will before the war is over.'

'A pile of blankets, coats and other articles of clothing had now come up from inside *UB-44* and the ship-wrecked sailors accepted them with eagerness. The medical supplies followed and, as a parting gesture of friendship, Bergman handed over two bottles of Schnapps. It was almost like an exchange of gifts between old friends and Captain Wilkinson was anxious to reciprocate. Someone found a half-empty packet of Player's cigarettes, passed them up to him and he handed them gravely to the U-Boat commander as a token of appreciation.

Konrad took them with equal solemnity. He didn't smoke himself. But he remembered that Hans enjoyed English cigarettes.

The motor dory started its engines and the two seamen holding the boathooks gave her a parting shove to help her on her way. Bergman climbed back on to the conning-tower and watched as the overcrowded motor-boat swung her bows in the direction of Norway and set off in pursuit of the two oared lifeboats that had long since passed over the horizon. He continued to watch in silence for several minutes wondering to himself whether the woman, and the men with her, would ever reach the Norwegian coast. It was an aspect of war he had never experienced or thought about before. And it was one he had little stomach for.

As the dory dwindled to a small black dot in the grey wastes of the sea he brought his mind back to the task in hand – the destruction of the now deserted and abandoned freighter.

'Finish her off, Essen,' he said quietly. 'Five rounds along the waterline should do the trick.'

The 3.5-inch opened a slow and deliberate fire and the Krupp shells punctured a neat row of holes along the red-painted waterline. But *Haven Court* seemed strangely reluctant to sink.

'Looks as though we need to put a torpedo into her, sir,' Bauer suggested.

While he was not anxious to waste an expensive tin fish on a sitting target Bergman had to bear in mind that they had been surfaced for more than an hour and, following the freighter's distress call, retribution in the shape of a British patrol ship or perhaps an aircraft was probably only just over the horizon. But at least it would give the crew some torpedo practice. And it would be a satisfying sensation to put a torpedo into a real live ship instead of a target dummy.

'We'll stay on the surface – it will be easier to spot any errors in aim that way,' he told Bauer. He walked across to the voicepipes. 'Flood up bow tubes. Set depth valves for 10 feet.' He waited while his orders were carried out.

'All forward tubes flooded, sir. Ready for firing.'

Haven Court, listing slightly where the shells had ripped open her hull, moved sluggishly with the wind and Bergman estimated her speed to be not more than 2 knots. *UB-44* was also motionless with her bows at 90° to the freighter's beam. The distance between them was only a thousand yards and no one but a blind man could miss at such a range. He bent down in front of the fixed sight in the centre of the bridge and squinted along the open tube to confirm the angle.

'Fire Bow One!'

UB-44 lurched softly as one of the new electric torpedoes shot from its tube and Bergman heard the tanks being flooded up to restore trim in compensation for the sudden loss of 3,334 lbs deadweight which the torpedo represented. Standing beside Bauer he watched the almost invisible wake of the *Type G-7e Mk III* streak for its target. It was holding an impeccable course that promised to strike *Haven Court* dead centre.

Fifty yards . . . thirty yards . . . twenty . . . ten.

He braced his hands on the rail in anticipation of the inevitable explosion. But nothing happened. The torpedo passed directly beneath the freighter but, for some inexplicable reason, the magnetic influence pistol in its nose failed to detonate the 660 lbs of explosive in the warhead.

'What the hell happened, Number One?'

'Must be a dud, sir. I could swear you didn't miss.'

'I should bloody well hope not at this range. Perhaps the target doesn't draw so much water as I thought and it was running too deep. What draught did it give in the book?'

'Fifteen feet deep-laden, sir.'

Bergman stared at the target as if hoping for inspiration. But none came and he shrugged his shoulders. Perhaps the first torpedo *had* been a dud.

'Fire Bow Two!'

Again the lurch, counterflooding to restore trim, and the faint almost invisible track arrowing towards the drifting steamer. And again, even though they saw the torpedo strike against the ship and then bounce angrily down the side to vanish astern, there was no explosion.

'Fire Bow Three!'

This time the torpedo behaved exactly as the instruction book said it should. There was a sudden almighty detonation which threw a column of water mast-high and *UB-44* reeled under the shock wave of the explosion. As the smoke and water cleared Bergman could see *Haven Court* slipping sideways with the sea pouring into the gaping hole torn in her keel plates. Soon she was lying horizontally with her funnel resting on the water and then, shortly after a shuddering internal explosion as the boilers blew up, she plunged beneath the waves.

Bergman derived little satisfaction from her destruction. In fact it caused him almost physical pain to see another ship destroyed so thoroughly. And, as he stared at the empty sea, he thought of the three small boats struggling to make landfall on the Norwegian coast before the weather broke. The stark realities of war were proving to be somewhat different from the romantic dreams of his youth. But it was too late to change his destiny now.

Doenitz himself was waiting at the quay as *UB-44* slid alongside at the end of her patrol. The anchor party in the bows stood smartly to attention while Bergman, Bauer and the other men on the bridge saluted. They looked tired, grey faced, unwashed and unshaven. Three weeks of unrewarding patrol in the North Sea had taken its inevitable toll of their stamina and every man in the crew was dreaming of fresh food, clean white sheets and the luxury of a hot bath.

Bergman was the first down the gangway and the *Kommodore* greeted him with a firm and understanding handshake.

'Congratulations on your first ship, *Herr Oberleutnant*. I'm sure *UB-44* will have many more to her credit before long.'

'Thank you, sir. But we would have bagged at least one more if the torpedoes had not failed to detonate.'

The expression on the *Kommodore's* face indicated that he had heard it all before. 'You were not the only one to suffer torpedo failures, Bergman. Kretschmer, Prien and most of the other commanders have told me a similar story. In fact I have called for a Special Inquiry to investigate the cause of the fault so we should get the bugs ironed out within a few days. Meanwhile each U-Boat will carry 50% of the old pattern *G-7s* in its outfit until we have got to the bottom of the trouble. Make sure you give your Flotilla Commander full details in your report. I will see that it is added to the evidence I am gathering for the Committee.'

He saluted gravely, significantly omitting the usual Nazi form of salute, and returned to his staff car. Bergman watched him drive away and then, having handed over to Bauer, he made his way to the Flotilla Office.

Kapitan Walther listened to his report without comment and, when Konrad had completed his de-briefing routine, he invited him to sit down.

'You can rest assured that the torpedo problem will be solved without delay. The *Kommodore* is furious with the Technical Branch and is threatening to make a personal report to the Fuehrer. So far as our own specialists can ascertain the magnetic influence pistols are faulty with the result that the torpedoes fail to explode. As a temporary measure they are fitting the old type conventional contact pistols to all weapons, including the *Type G-7e,* until the boffins have produced a solution.'

'How did *U-47* get on at Scapa Flow, sir?' Bergman had been dying to find out ever since *UB-44* had tied up at Pier G.

Walther shook his head. 'I'm afraid the fog beat Prien just as it defeated you. But we haven't given up the plan. You'll both be given the chance of another stab at it later on.'

Konrad smiled his thanks but he was careful to conceal his lack of enthusiasm for the project. In his view it was still a stupid idea with the risks heavily outweighing the gains.

'We've had several notable successes while you've been away,' Walther continued. 'Schuhardt and *U-29* sank a

British aircraft carrier last week* and *U-39* nearly got the *Ark Royal*.' †

'I'm glad *someone's* been lucky,' Bergman said wearily. 'Will it be all right to grant the men a spot of leave?'

'Of course. *UB-44* is likely to be at base for fourteen days at least. Seven days for each Watch should be sufficient. But I can only spare *you* for a short period so I'm afraid a long week-end will have to suffice. BDU wants you to look after the paperwork for the Committee of Inquiry into the torpedo failures. Incidentally, Kirchen's due back today so I daresay you can organize something between you for the weekend.'

Kapitan Walther's offer of leave was just the tonic Bergman needed after the strains and frustrations of the previous few weeks. *And* he wasn't exactly looking forward to acting as office-boy to the torpedo committee. Not that he had much say in the organization of his brief spell of freedom. Hans was a day late in arriving back at base due to the thick fogs that had closed down over the North Sea but, undeterred, he burst on Wilhelmshaven with typical exuberance. He found Konrad sitting quietly in the *Kommando* Room reading the newspapers in a belated effort to catch up on the war news and dragged him protestingly into his white SSK Mercedes.

'Hurry up, Kon. We've only been given two days and I want to make the most of it. How about Kiel? We haven't been there since we left the Periscope School. I wonder if Greta's still behind the bar at the Berlinhoff?'

Bergman sank back into the taut leather bucket seat with a sigh. His hopes of a few quiet days were shattered by the

*HMS *Courageous* was sunk in the Channel on 17 September, 1939, with the loss of 578 officers and men.

†*U-39* was sunk by the British destroyers *Faulknor*, *Foxhound* and *Firedrake*, on 14 September, after an abortive attack on the *Ark Royal*. *U-39* was the first U-boat to be sunk during the war although most of her crew were picked up.

raucous roar that emerged from the Mercedes' twin exhausts as Hans gunned the engine to life. 'God knows where he gets the petrol from to run this thing,' he thought to himself. Doubtlessly Kirchen Senior's influence in the Party had something to do with it.

'Hang on to your hat, Kon. We're heading for the bright lights!'

'I doubt it. Don't forget there's a black-out.'

'Fine — then they won't be able to see what we get up to.'

They were in Kiel by early evening and having booked in at a hotel — an apparently simple task with Kirchen's connections — they found themselves comfortably seated in the bar of the Berlinerhoff in time for dinner.

'I suppose you realize they turned a bloody rear-admiral out of that room so that we could have it,' Konrad pointed out as their first drinks arrived.

Hans grinned wickedly. 'Serves him right. The old bastard ought to be at sea like the rest of us.' He picked up the menu and studied it.

The stringencies of rationing precluded the more exotic dishes they had enjoyed at the Berlinerhoff in pre-war days but the meal was well-cooked if somewhat uninspiring. They ate quietly and Bergman began feeling puzzled by Kirchen's sudden lack of verve.

'What's up? Been having trouble with your torpedoes?'

'Haven't we all?' Hans answered cryptically. 'No, it isn't that. I was just thinking of that Polish girl I had dinner with here last year. You remember — Wanda. She lived in Warsaw. I wonder what's happened to her now?'

'I expect she's all right,' Bergman said trying to cheer him up. 'I know the Luftwaffe smashed Warsaw up but I don't suppose it's quite so bad as the radio reports make out.'

'I wasn't thinking about that — I doubt if she was in Warsaw in any case. The family have a big estate in eastern Poland. I was wondering what the Russians did to her when they took over. Poor bitch.'

'You've been reading too many horror stories about the Red Terror,' Konrad said soothingly. 'Red rape and rivers of blood only exist in the minds of the journalists who write the rubbish. It's not that bad really, you know.'

'Take it from me, Kon, it *is.*' For once in his life Kirchen was deadly serious. 'Some of my family got caught in the Revolution and I *know.* If there was one thing I agreed with Hitler over it was his anti-Bolshevik policy. And now look what's happened – Stalin's our bloody ally ! I never did have a high opinion of Adolf's intelligence but that non-aggression pact just about finished me.'

'I won't disagree with you.' Konrad sensed that Hans meant what he said for once. 'But I'll tell you one thing. Whichever side Stalin ends up on is going to win this war – so I'd rather it was ours.'

Kirchen sank his kummel and looked at his companion sharply.

'What's this sudden change of tune, Kon? I can remember that night we were in Willi's Bar with Vargas when you were singing Hitler's praises for saving Germany from the menace of communism. Now you can't wait to throw yourself into Uncle Joe's arms.'

Konrad remembered the talks he had had with Rahel – talks that had lasted deep into the night. But then neither Hans nor anyone else knew about Rahel or their relationship. And, even if he *had* known, he would not have understood it for, to Kirchen, a woman only existed for one purpose – to satisfy his physical needs. Hans should have been a muslim. The strong liqueurs after three weeks of abstinence were going to Bergman's head. He could just imagine Hans sitting on a camel dressed as a sheikh. He began to grin. The mental picture became more ridiculous the more he embellished it and he suddenly laughed aloud.

'What's so funny?' Kirchen demanded.

Konrad restrained his giggles with difficulty. The alcohol was beginning to make his head swim.

'Nothing, nothing important,' he said. 'But thinking of me as a communist, it's almost like considering you a Nazi.'

It was Hans' turn to laugh. But there was a forced hollowness to the sound. Intuitively he sensed that he had inadvertently touched a tender spot and, ordering two more glasses of kummel, he changed the subject.

'Did you hear about Kretschmer torpedoing the *Nelson*?' Bergman whistled with admiration.

'He didn't?'

'Too right he didn't – but Goebbels didn't find out in time to stop Joyce* from telling the British public that the glorious German Navy had sunk their most famous battleship.'

'I missed all this while I was at sea. What happened?'

Hans lit one of Captain Wilkinson's cigarettes which Konrad had given him while they were driving to Kiel.

'It was like this. Otto was on patrol somewhere off the Scottish coast and he thought he saw a big fat target in his sights. It was a pitch black night and all he could make out was this enormous shadow so, being Otto, he fired a torpedo. He hit it all right but, when it exploded, he realized that he'd fired at a large rock sticking up out of the sea. So, seeing the funny side of it, he radioed a signal to BDU saying '*Felson* torpedoed but not sunk.' † But some silly clot at Wilhelmshaven misread the message as "*Nelson* torpedoed but not sunk." Naturally Goebbels' propaganda ministry went wild when they got the news and no one knew about the mistake until Kretschmer got back to base. You can imagine Doenitz's face when he found out – and I hate to think what the *Herr Doktor* had to say.' ‡

---

*William Joyce, an ex-patriate Englishman known as Lord Haw-Haw, who broadcast German propaganda from Berlin during the war.

†*Felson* is German for rock.

‡This is a true story. See *The Golden Horseshoe*, the biography of Otto Kretschmer, by Terence Robertson.

Konrad enjoyed the joke. He was beginning to feel better. There was no doubt about it – Hans was just the tonic he needed after a frustrating patrol. He emptied his glass.

Kirchen glanced across the dining room at a couple of hostesses sitting at a table near the orchestra. He gave them one of his famous smiles. Both girls responded. Aside from their professional interest personal curiosity gave their answering smiles an unexpected warmth. After the succession of dreary business men and fusty old Army pensioners who frequented the Berlinerhoff now that the war had dragged off the younger and more interesting element the two handsome and smartly uniformed naval officers looked decidedly attractive. And, as a business proposition, they might even have money as well.

Hans nudged Bergman as the girls came over to their table.

'We're going to be all right tonight, Kon. Just what I need after three weeks in a cold damp bunk. You take the blonde – I'll have the one with the big knockers.'

Konrad found himself thinking of Rahel as the two hostesses joined them. But the need that stirred in his loins after nearly a month at sea quickly overcame his doubts. And, as he well knew, it wasn't like that with Rahel anyway. They were just good friends – no more, no less.

Hans summoned the waiter as the girls sat down and ordered a bottle of champagne. It was blatantly obvious that he had already got the whole thing organized. So, whether Konrad fancied the blonde girl or not, he was left with no room to escape. And, studying her face and trimly sensual body while Kirchen popped the cork, he had to admit to himself that he *did* fancy her. Pushing his thoughts of Rahel to the back of his mind Bergman picked up the glass of champagne and settled down to enjoy whatever the night might bring. Life was too short to worry.

Gerda lived up to the promise of his first impression. Behind the locked door of the hotel bedroom they came together with an impact that matched the fierceness of a torpedo penetrating the unprotected vitals of a helpless victim. And as the image flashed across his mind something made Bergman look down at the girl spread nakedly beneath him. Gerda's nipples pointed up at him like pink accusing fingers and he had a sudden mental picture of the woman in the lifeboat – the pale white skin tinged with blue as the chill morning air ate into her bones, the big frightened eyes and those nipples, taut with cold under the flimsy nightgown, pointing towards him in mute accusation. He shivered at the memory.

The alcohol sitting sourly in his stomach made him feel sick but he forced himself to look again in a blurred effort to destroy the image that had haunted him continuously since the day he had sunk the *Haven Court*. A face smiled up at him from the rumpled pillow. The room spun with sickening violence and he could feel his body trembling with reaction. God! he was going mad – the face staring up at him from the pillow was that of Rahel.

The shock brought him back to reality with shattering abruptness. He looked around the sordid little hotel room, at the sex-rumpled bed on which he was kneeling, at the naked body of the woman beneath him. Why Rahel? And why now? Gerda's blonde head lifted and her arms reached out towards him. Konrad wrenched away in disgust.

He began pulling on his clothes. Gerda sat up in bed staring at him as if he had gone mad. Well, perhaps he had. How could he think of Rahel when he was sleeping with another woman – when he was capable of sending yet another to die of exposure in an open boat. He pushed the ends of his shirt into the waistband of his trousers and fastened the buttons. His fingers were still trembling but he felt calmer as he grappled with the questions that throbbed in his brain.

Was there a deeper involvement with Rahel than he had realized? It was impossible. Rahel Yousoff had Jewish blood

120

in her veins and such an involvement in Nazi Germany was tantamount to professional suicide – and Bergman's instinct for survival was too great to countenance such a personal sacrifice. And yet, deep down, he wasn't quite so sure.

Digging into his pocket he found a bundle of banknotes, peeled off twenty and threw them at Gerda. Then, mumbling an incoherent apology, he hurried out of the room, stumbled down the hotel stairs, and stepped out into the blacked-out streets of Kiel.

He found a cheap bar near the harbour and got deeply and gloriously drunk. It seemed the only solution.

CHAPTER SEVEN

Bergman rested his elbows on the ledge of the conning-tower and stared broodingly at the grey seas streaming down the side of the U-boat as they headed nor'nor'west across the dismal wastes of the North Sea. He hated the war. He hated *UB-44*. But most of all he hated himself and what he had become. Everyone, it seemed, was blessed with luck except himself.

Guther Prien had achieved the impossible and stormed Scapa Flow on the night of 14 October – succeeding where both of them had failed a month before. Not that he grudged Prien his triumph. It took guts to do what he had done and Bergman felt sure that his own courage was inadequate to carry out such a feat.*

Kirchen, too, had scored a resounding success off the Norwegian coast a few days later when he bagged a 10,000 ton County Class cruiser and then survived a devastating twelve hour depth-charge attack by no less than four destroyers. His new boat, *UB-203*, had been badly smashed but somehow he had pulled her through. And it went without saying that he had received a hero's welcome when he limped back into Wilhelmshaven. 'He's down for an Iron Cross (1st Class) at least,' Konrad thought bitterly. But that was typical of Hans. Whatever happened, and whatever the circumstances, he always came out on top.

And it wasn't only the U-boats. The pocket-battleships were also having a field day. *Graf Spee*, hunting the South Atlantic, was snapping up freighters and tankers by the

---

*Prien's attack was a classic of submarine warfare. Entering the heavily defended anchorage at night he sank the battleship *Royal Oak* (29,150 tons). The outstanding feature of his epic feat was the fact that he took *U-47* into the Flow *on the surface*.

dozen while more than fifty major ships of the Royal Navy were frantically chasing their tails in a vain attempt to locate her and bring her to battle. *Koenig,* too, was going well. Operating along the crowded shipping lanes of the North Atlantic, and hiding herself away amongst the ice floes of the Denmark Strait when things got too hot, she had already sunk over 100,000 tons of British shipping and seemed set fair to double this tally before returning to base. He wondered whether that old devil von Mikel had forgotten about the exchange of signals yet. And, for the first time in three days, he grinned quietly to himself as he recalled his impudent farewell when *Koenig's* captain had eavesdropped on his conversation with Meyer.

'Thought you'd like something to warm you up, sir.'

Bergman looked down at the tin mug which Herzog thrust into his hands and caught the aroma of rich sweet coffee.

'Thank you, Chief. Just what I needed.' The hot liquid burned his mouth as he gulped it down but the heat glowed satisfyingly in his stomach as he began to feel better. He glanced at his watch. 'You're not on Duty Watch, surely?'

'No, sir. But we were just brewing up in the PO mess and I thought you'd like some. And, begging your pardon, sir, neither are you – unless you're trying to get pneumonia or something.'

Bergman sighed.

'You're quite right, Chief. I just came up on the bridge to blow a few cobwebs out of my mind.'

Herzog grinned sympathetically. Highly coloured stories of how Bergman and Kirchen had become involved in a mass orgy in Kiel were rife among *UB-44's* crew, although how they started was difficult to tell.

'If it's a woman you're thinking about, sir, I'd forget it if I were you. There's plenty more on the beach – especially when you're wearing a U-Boat uniform.'

Bergman did not answer and the old Warrant Officer suddenly remembered the signal received from BDU earlier in the day – a confirmation report, gleaned from Lloyds and sent on by an agent in New York, that the Anglo-Norge Line steamer *Haven Court* had been sunk by an unidentified U-boat. And that only one of the ship's boats had reached land, with but a single survivor, an Irish stoker named Kelly.

'If you're thinking about the boat we sank on our last patrol . . .' Herzog searched for the right words. 'I sailed with von Arnauld in the last war and he used to feel the same way as you, sir. It would be all right sinking ships provided nobody got killed. And he was probably the greatest U-Boat commander of all time.'

Bergman knew what Herzog was trying to do and he appreciated it. But *Haven Court* and its victims no longer haunted his thoughts. He had done all he could and his conscience was clear. And, to Konrad, *that* was sufficient. No, what was bothering him was the change in his relationship with Rahel and the problems that followed – problems with which he had not been trained to cope.

With the unerring instinct of the veteran sailor Herzog sensed the cause of his skipper's moody silence. It was difficult to put into words and it was not exactly the sort of thing a man could say openly in these days – not even in a U-boat.

'Last time, sir, in the '14-'18 affair, we had the Kaiser in charge but all of us knew that, at the bottom of it, we were fighting for Germany. And this time, sir, we've got Hitler running the show – but we're still fighting for the same thing. We don't fight wars to keep governments in power. We fight them to save our country from the enemy.'

'True, Herzog, very true. But I don't think it wise to voice your views to too many people – they might be misinterpreted. Now get below like a good chap and have some rest.'

The Cox'n grinned cheerfully as he departed down the conning-tower ladder clutching the empty tin mug. The Old Man was a real tight one, he decided. He'd come out with it as far as he'd dared and yet Bergman had carefully avoided committing himself to the trap. Well, time alone would tell. But he knew which interpretation he'd put *his* money on.

The diving klaxon screamed while he was still on his way down and the coxswain jumped the last few feet into the control room to clear the ladder for the men clambering down from the deck. Bauer, alert as always, was already at his post in front of the Diving Table and orders passed crisply up and down the U-boat as the lookouts, resembling weird prehistoric marine animals in their black oilskins, tumbled into the crowded control area.

'Clutches out – switches on. Group up, full ahead both. Close main vents and flood all tanks. Hydroplanes to dive.'

Herzog reached up and slid the dog catches of the lower hatch as Bergman dropped down into the ordered chaos of the control room. Every second counted.

'British cruiser and two destroyers coming up from the south-east,' Konrad told Bauer breathlessly as he threw off his leather coat and pulled off his heavy sea boots. 'Moving fast but we should be in a perfect attack position.'

'Up periscope.'

The tube rose smoothly and silently and Bergman squeezed the handles with excitement. After two failures he dare not let this chance slip through his fingers. He peered into the glass searching for his targets. A wave sloshed over the hooded upper lens and he swore as the water temporarily obscured his vision. At the risk of betraying *UB-44*'s presence he raised the stalk of the 'scope a further two feet to clear the choppy waves.

'Target bearing 190. Range 10 miles. I am 10 degrees on his starboard bow – estimated target speed 25 knots. Down 'scope.'

Bauer translated the hurriedly snatched information on to the *Torpedorechner* – a primitive form of mechanical slide-rule and computer that converted the three variables of bearing, range, and speed into an attack angle. The machine helped to take the guesswork out of an attack plot but its accuracy depended entirely on the information fed into it by the experienced eye of the U-boat commander at the periscope. Only he could see what was happening on the surface. And it was on his judgement of range, speed and bearing that a successful attack depended.

Herzog, still clutching the empty tin mug, watched in silence. No one was allowed to speak during an attack run. But as he saw Bergman crouched expectantly at the periscope memories of the good old days of 1917 came crowding back into his mind. He felt 20 years younger and, unlike the rest, of the greenhorns crammed into the control room, his heart-beat was steady and regular. Pulling rank, he took over the task of steering from Weisbad who, at 19, was, in his view, too young for such responsibility. Nothing must be allowed to happen that might let the skipper down.

'Up periscope . . . bearing 170. Range 8 miles. I am now 12 degrees on his starboard bow. Down periscope.'

The pilot glanced down at the scribbled figures on the chart. 'I make the speed 30 knots, sir.'

Bergman nodded. The confirmation was useful.

'It's going to be tricky.' He glanced at Bauer. 'Have you got a DA yet, Number One?'

'DA Green 12, sir.'

'Good – recheck on next periscope report.' He spoke into the microphone hanging down beside the periscope. 'Blow torpedo room? Set for fifteen feet and flood up all tubes.'

There was a pause as the torpedoes were set for the re-quired running depth. Then *Torpedo-obergefreiter* Peder-sen's voice reported back over the intercom.

'Torpedoes set for 15 feet – tubes flooding up . . . Tube 1 flooded . . . all tubes flooded and ready, sir.'

'Up periscope!' Another quick survey. 'Bearing 165 . . . range 7 miles . . . angle to bow 14 degrees. Down periscope.'

Could do with more bow angle, thought Bergman. If we come in too fine the target area will be too small.

'Helmsman, starboard 10.'

'Starboard 10, sir.'

'Reduce to half speed.'

'Group down . . . half speed it is, sir.'

Bergman was surprised to find he was still ice cool. The intense concentration required to manoeuvre *UB-44* into the attack position had pushed all thoughts of danger from his mind. And he was enjoying the thrill of the hunt.

The course change and reduction in speed had complicated Bauer's work on his machine but he corrected the reading with the uncanny speed of a Chinese abacus operator. His voice sounded unsteady with excitement.

'Deflection angle zero, sir.'

This was where the skipper's skill showed up. An awkward fast-moving target, three quick peeks through the periscope, a slight variation of speed and direction and, presto, there was no need for an aim-off. It was almost like an artillery gunner firing over open sights – and as satisfyingly dangerous.

Bergman walked over to the charts and stared down at Hauptmann's plot. He looked at it in silence for a few moments translating the scene he had observed on the surface on to the white paper with its thin pencil lines and neatly circled figures. Then, his decision made, he moved back beside Bauer.

'The destroyers are about two miles abeam the main target. They're moving too fast to operate their ASDIC detectors so they probably haven't spotted us. I intend to fire at 1,000 yards so that means we've got to get inside that screen.'

Herzog, sitting upright at the wheel with his eyes fixed on the vital needle of the gyro repeater, overheard Bergman's decision and sucked his teeth expectantly. Perhaps the others didn't realize what he meant. But the old coxswain could still vividly remember being caught in a similar situation while serving with von Arnauld in *U-135*. Once inside the steel cordon of destroyers the U-Boat was at the enemy's mercy like a salmon trapped inside a fisherman's net and frantically swimming in circles seeking for an escape that wasn't there.

'Up periscope.'

Bergman called off the data to Bauer and made his final calculations. The destroyers seemed to be almost on top of them and he had to remind himself that the magnification of the attack lens he was using had the effect of diminishing distances.

'Down periscope!' This was it. 'Take her to 70 feet.'

'Planes to dive. Holding half speed, sir. Course 1-8-0.'

He felt *UB-44* angle downwards and he mentally calculated the speed adjustment necessary to compensate for the dive.

'Planes amidships – holding level trim, sir. 70 feet and steady.'

They were fully committed. There was no more he could do. Only when they climbed back to periscope depth would he know if his calculations were correct. And if they weren't they would probably be run down by one of the destroyers. It didn't bear thinking about. He reached for the microphone again.

'Bow torpedo room.'

'Bow torpedo room, sir.'

'We won't have time to aim each shot individually so we'll have to fire a salvo spread. I want a one second delay between each shot and a one degree starboard deflection in sequence. No 1 – zero; No 2 + 1, No 3 + 2, No 4 + 3. Check.'

Pedersen repeated the instructions back. Konrad glanced down at the stopwatch clenched in his right hand. They should be clear of the screen now. He felt the tension mounting.

'Hold the bloody thing straight, Essen,' he shouted.

Essen saw the inclometer dip and correct fractionally. Probably a layer of cold water affecting the density of the sea and upsetting the trim. He flooded up No 7 tank and levelled her gently. His face shone with sweat. Herzog, hunched forward over the helm, shifted his hands fractionally to hold *UB-44* on course.

'Bring her up to 30 feet!'

'Planes up – level at 30!' The U-boat angled towards the surface with every eye fastened on the quivering red needle of the depth-gauge.

' 'midship planes. 30 feet and level, sir.'

Bergman stared at the stopwatch. This was the crucial test of his skill. A thirty second burst at full speed should just compensate exactly for the distance lost during the shallow dive under the destroyer screen.

'Full ahead both!'

'Group up. Full ahead both, sir.'

The hum of the electric motors increased in pitch and the lamps flickered for a brief second before the compensators switched circuits. 20 . . . 15 . . . 10 . . . 5.

'Half speed.'

'Group down, half ahead both.'

'Torpedo room stand by. Up periscope.'

The column hissed upwards. Now a quick check to make sure that the target had not changed course. A final judgement of the range. And then! Bergman stepped forward slowly as if savouring the moment of triumph. The stopwatch dangled from the string around his neck and his cap was twisted sideways to avoid contact with the periscope. Reaching forward with steady hands, he grasped the two handles and pushed his eye up against the circular aperture. He felt like Pandora preparing to open her box as he peered into the lens.

'*Shit*!'

HMS *Salisbury* was zig-zagging. And, against all expectations, Bergman found himself staring at the cruiser's high sloping stern instead of her broadside. The adrenalin pumped into his system as he absorbed the shock. No chance of a shot at this angle. But was the cruiser beginning the leg of a zig-zag or nearing the end and about to change course again? To hell with the risk of keeping the periscope showing above the surface. *He had to know.*

Bergman watched intently as he evaluated her speed and range. No problems there. If only the cruiser would turn.

High up on the bridge of HMS *Salisbury* Leading Seaman Parker tightened his fingers round the spokes of the helm as he watched the zig-zag indicator clock. The hand crawled around with irritating slowness but Parker waited with stoic patience. As it reached the upper segment he pushed the wheel round to pick up the new course. There was a maddening delay before the ship responded to the rudder but then, slowly and majestically, she began to turn, swinging her bows across the arc of the horizon as she heeled obediently to the helm.

Bergman saw her begin to come around and he grinned with elation. Just a small correction.

'Port 5.'

Herzog mirrored Parker's movement in the reverse direction. 'Port 5, sir.'

' 'midships helm. Stand by for salvo firing . . . FIRE!'

UB-44 shuddered at one second intervals as the torpedoes shot from their tubes and Essen carefully watched the trim as Pedersen and his men closed the bow doors and pumped the tubes clear of water. He flooded up No 6 and No 10 tanks to compensate for the loss of weight, checked his trim again, and waited further orders.

'Torpedoes running, sir.'

Bergman acknowledged the hydrophone operator's report with a nod. He snapped the periscope handles upwards.

'Down periscope. Take her to 100 feet, Number One.'

'Planes to dive. Group up. 100 feet and level.'

UB-44's bows went down and the extra surge of power from the electric motors forced her towards the bottom like a pike swooping on its prey. The depth-indicators swung down rapidly and Bauer ordered the planes into the horizontal position as they touched the 95 feet calibration. The U-boat levelled out and held her trim in the dark depths of the ocean like a replete shark sinking complacently to the bottom to digest a hurriedly snatched meal.

'Stop engines.'

The low hum of the motors faded and the cramped interior of the submarine was silent save for the slither of rubber-soled shoes on bare steel floors and the steady monotonous drip of water. Bergman looked down at his stopwatch.

'I estimate a torpedo run of not more than 90 seconds, Number One. That leaves us with exactly 30 seconds to wait from now.'

Instinctively Bauer raised his head and stared up at the curving steel roof of their underwater vault as if watching the torpedoes racing through the water towards their target. Herzog chewed his thumbnail and grinned. 'Your eyes are no good in a U-boat, mate,' he thought to himself. 'It's *ears* that count. You might as well be a blind man when you're cooped up in one of these sardine cans.' He continued to chew the nail ruminatively.

'Ten seconds.'

Every man tensed with anticipation as the seconds ticked away. It was as if the entire crew were holding their breaths. And most of them were.

'Five . . . four . . . three.'

Crum-m-mp!

'It's a hit!' shouted Bauer. Disregarding discipline, he thumped Bergman on the back with his fist in his excitement. Someone began to cheer and the others took it up. But Konrad did not join in the jubilation. One torpedo hit was not enough to sink a cruiser. And he wanted a kill!

Surely *all* the other three hadn't missed.

A vicious clap of thunder cracked with a force that hurt their ears and then rumbled on angrily. *UB-44* lurched sideways as the concussion struck her and the men cursed as they were thrown to the floor.

'Depth bombs!' someone yelled.

'Silence! We're quite safe,' Bergman shouted. 'That wasn't a depth-charge. Get back to your posts.'

The men scrambled to their feet and returned to their places sheepishly – ashamed of the sudden panic that had gripped them as the hollow boom of the explosion echoed through the submarine.

Bergman's expression was calm and assured although he could scarcely repress the excitement pounding through his veins. Bauer's face was split in a wide grin of triumph. But, like Konrad, he was reluctant to say what was in his mind. He turned to Herzog who was still sitting at the helm chewing his thumbnail with total lack of concern.

'You've seen plenty of U-boat action, Cox'n. I don't know what *you* *t*hink but *I'd* say we hit the magazine and she's blown up.'

Herzog's teeth carefully trimmed off the nail. 'Aye,' he said with an irritating lack of interest, 'it sounded very much like that to me too.' But it was impossible to maintain a straight face any longer. He chuckled deep down in his throat like an asthmatic bull-frog. 'I *knew* you'd pull it off this trip, skipper.'

Bergman's personal feelings of triumph were more than balanced by the realization that, if the attack had been a success, the British would not rest until they had smashed the U-boat into a buckled wreck. His fears were quickly realized.

Crump! Crum-m-p!

'Now I'd say *they* were depth-bombs,' Herzog observed quietly. Then, ignoring the explosions, he began chewing his index finger.

Bergman reached for the microphone.

'This is the captain. *UB-44* has almost certainly sunk a British Town-class cruiser and we are now coming under depth-charge attack. We may be pinned down for twelve hours or more so I want everyone to conserve air and remain absolutely quiet. We shall shake them off in the finish.'

The calm confident tone of his voice had the required effect. The men off duty settled back on their bunks while those on Watch remained quietly at their stations ready to obey whatever order they received. Bergman and Bauer sat down on the control room floor and leaned their backs against the steel bulkhead.

Two destroyers – say about fifty depth-charges for each – that meant a hundred chances of being crippled. Konrad weighed the odds carefully. The first two explosions were a good distance away so they obviously hadn't been located yet. Until the enemy got a firm ASDIC fix on *UB-44* they were in the position of a blind man hunting for a needle in a haystack. And, of course, they were probably searching outside the screen instead of inside.

The detonations continued at irregular intervals as the destroyers tried to flush them out. But they were far enough away not to present any immediate danger.

Another crump and the U-boat heeled slightly but quickly righted herself. The lights were still on and there were no signs of damage. Bergman picked up a book and began to read it in an effort to set an example to the men.

Another blast shook the U-Boat. *That* was too bloody close for comfort. But *UB-44* was still showing no ill-effects from the pounding. He glanced around the control room studying the faces of the men. They were sweating but they looked calm enough. Two more violent explosions rocked the boat and a light bulb shattered with the concussion. He turned over the page of his book and continued reading.

Herzog started chewing his other hand. He'd been through worse depth-charge attacks than this and he wasn't unduly alarmed. Good to see the skipper setting an example – one or two of the younger men had been looking frightened. Pity the Old Man was holding his book upside down though – it rather spoiled the effect. But he doubted whether anyone else had noticed.

Suddenly something struck the outer casing of the U-boat's hull with a giant hammer. At least, that was what it sounded like. *UB-44* jerked like a stuck pig and the lights went out. There was an ominous sound of water flooding into the boat and men groped in the darkness. *Machinenobermaat* Hoffmann located the fuse box, switched on the low power emergency lighting and began tracing the damaged circuit. Two other engineers came through from the motor room to help.

Bergman was on his feet immediately the depth-charge exploded and, as the dim glow of the emergency lamps flickered to life, he quickly surveyed the chaos of the control room.

CRUM-M-P! CRUM-M-P! CRUMP!

UB-44 rocked wildly with the blasts. Men slithered on the wet steel plating, lost their balance, and fell in cursing heaps of tangled arms and legs. Others, caught unawares, were slammed against the unyielding bulkheads with a force that stunned them momentarily.

'Flood down to 200 feet,' Bergman ordered. It was a gamble, especially if the depth-charges had weakened the hull. But he had to escape from the lethal cascade of explosive canisters that threatened their utter destruction at any second. 'Damage control parties report please. Maintain silence.'

The valves opened to admit more water to the ballast tanks and *UB-44* dropped a further 100 feet under the increased weight. Groping through the dim twilight, their torches checking for broken pipes and leaking plates, the Damage Control Parties searched every inch of the submarine.

'Forward DCP reporting, sir. Some leaks in the high pressure air lines but we're fixing them. No water inside the boat.'

'Aft DCP reporting, sir. Two sprung plates in No 6 compartment. Leaking badly but the pumps will hold it. Emergency repairs in hand.'

'Negative pumps!' Bergman's decision was firm and immediate. 'If the enemy sound detectors hear the pumps they'll have us pin-pointed. Let the water drain away into the bilges.' He turned to Bauer. 'Get along and see how bad it is, Number One.' Bauer nodded, grabbed a torch from the rack, and hurried aft.

'Midship's Party – report please.'

'Engine room sound, sir, but the Chief thinks the starboard main bearing is strained. There's water coming in low down in the motor room.'

This was the most ominous damage yet; Bergman wanted more details.

'Keep it away from the batteries – and lift the covers to make sure there's no water down there.' Sea water mixing with the acid of the batteries would create chlorine gas – the most feared enemy of the U-boat crews. Whatever other risks had to be taken the salt water *must* be kept out of the battery compartments.

'Midship's DCP reporting, sir. The batteries are completely dry. Kornfeldt has rigged a canvas gutter under the leak and we're draining the water into the starboard bilge.'

The relief showed in Bergman's face as he heard the report. Well, they weren't dead yet. He began checking the readings on the cracked glass dials of the indicator gauges to hide the signs of strain from the crew.

'Depth-charge patterns have moved away, sir.'

Bergman paused in his self appointed task as Herzog reported. He listened carefully.

'About two miles, I'd say, sir,' the Coxswain added, standing with his head cocked curiously to one side.

Bergman nodded. They were in luck after all. The near

misses must have been blind flukes – chance shots as the avenging destroyers roared overhead scattering their charges at random. And, as if to confirm their escape, Hoffman and Korman's work on the fuse box paid dividends and the main lights suddenly came on with blinding brilliance. The mess inside the U-boat, now revealed in the harsh light, was indescribable, but Bergman no longer cared. To hell with that – providing the hull was still sound and the engines worked they could still make it.

It was now or never. While the enemy was hunting to the westward they might just be able to slip east and escape the net.

'Rig for silent running. Steer 090, Cox'n.'

UB-44 crept slowly east, inching her way through the black depths like an aquatic Red Indian stalking his prey, while Bergman and his men worked to restore some semblance of order inside the hull. After fifteen minutes he stopped motors and waited while the hydrophone operator checked for surface noises. There was nothing to report. Satisfied, he ordered the U-boat to thirty feet. She rose slowly, pausing every fifty feet for another nervewracking probe with the hydrophones.

'Thirty feet and level, sir. No reports of HE.'

'Up periscope.'

The column slid upwards and Bergman gripped the handles tightly to conceal his trembling hands as his eye pushed up against the lens. He moved swiftly through a complete circle of 360° followed by a sweep of the sky.

'The destroyers are about six miles away,' he announced over the loudspeakers. 'There is no sign of the cruiser but judging by the large oil slick and surface wreckage to the north I think we can claim a kill.'

There was no cheering this time – only smiles of satisfaction on weary oil-stained faces. They had been tested in the furnace of war and not found wanting. Now they were veterans. And veterans didn't cheer every success. It was just something to be shrugged off as another job well done.

Bergman experienced the same satisfaction. The men had been steady and resourceful in an emergency and no one had cracked up. More importantly *he* had not let them or *UB-44* down. And, from a purely selfish and personal point of view, he had evened his score with that of Hans Kirchen – one cruiser each.

'Stand by to surface.'

As Bergman stepped back to allow Bauer to supervise the surfacing routine he stubbed his toe against a hard metal object on the floor. He cursed and looked down.

For the first time in six hours he suddenly realized that his feet were completely bare and, casting his mind back, he remembered dragging off his sea boots when he first slid down into the control room after the initial enemy sighting report. He must have been in such a hurry that he'd ripped his socks off as well. Bergman smiled to himself. Well, at least he'd proved one thing today. He might have bare feet but, thank God, he'd shown that he didn't have *cold* feet.

CHAPTER EIGHT

UB-44's successful attack on the British cruiser was quickly exploited by the Nazi propaganda machine and, on his return to Germany, Bergman found the limelight of publicity both irritating and embarrassing. Radio interviews, VIP invitations to parties, and morale boosting speeches to the munitions workers of the Ruhr swallowed every second of available time. And although he managed to slip away for ten days' leave with his mother and step-father in Bavaria, his planned visit to Kiel to see Rahel – a trip that had to be kept secret for obvious reasons – failed to materialize due to his new-found fame.

He now ranked alongside U-boat heroes like Prien, Kretschmer, Schuard and Kirchen. And his previously sober blue uniform sparkled with decorations – the Submarine Insignia for the completion of three operational patrols; the Iron Cross (2nd Class), a standard medal awarded to the majority of submarine commanders; and the Iron Cross (1st Class) in recognition of his skill and resource in sinking the *Salisbury*.

But to Bergman they were mere baubles. As a career officer what pleased him far more was the third narrow gold ring on his sleeve denoting his promotion to *Kapitanleutnant*. That was tangible evidence that Doenitz and his superiors thought highly of his professional ability for, whatever decorations the Government might heap upon the men who brought honour and glory to the Nazi flag, the conservative admirals of the *Kriegsmarine* only promoted officers who measured up to their own demanding standards.

When he finally managed to snatch time for a brief visit to Kiel to see Rahel, however, he discovered another reason

138

for hating the blaze of publicity that had followed in the wake of his success.

She had never seen him in uniform and they had never discussed his work. She had a vague idea that he was connected with ship-building or marine engineering but she had never given the matter much thought. Their relationship was strangely remote and, on the odd occasions when they met, they spent most of their time discussing politics. She had found him kind and considerate but very correct. And, although it went no deeper than that, she was fond of him.

But now, with his picture splashed on the front page of every newspaper and his name recurring again and again on the radio, it was no longer possible to hide the fact that he was an officer in the *Kriegsmarine*. And when she saw him standing at the door in uniform she slammed it in his face. Konrad raised his hand to knock again. Then he changed his mind and walked slowly back down the street. He felt disappointed and bitter but he didn't blame her. Terrible things were happening in Germany, things that were for the most part carefully suppressed from public knowledge, but Bergman knew enough to hazard a guess at the truth.

When he returned to his cabin that night he lifted the official portrait of Hitler from its hook and slipped it into a drawer of his locker. Pulling open another drawer he took out a photograph of the Grunnenburg mountain and hung it carefully on the empty hook. From now on the picture would remind him why he was fighting the war. Not for Adolf Hitler. Nor for the Nazis or their monstrous creation, the Third Reich. But for Germany – the Germany of tall mountains and sweet scented pine forests – the country he loved. Then, opening a fresh bottle of Schnapps, he sat down and began thinking about Rahel. By midnight the bottle was empty.

'You're looking rather off-colour, Bergman,' Doenitz observed as he waved Konrad into a chair. 'There's a 'flu epidemic about – are you sure you're all right?'

'Yes thank you, sir,' Bergman lied. 'I was at a celebration last night with some friends.' The *Kommodore* did not approve of solitary drinkers and, in any case, he had no desire to draw attention to Rahel and their friendship. 'I'll be all right after lunch.'

Doenitz nodded sympathetically.

'Ah, yes, I understand. And allow me to take this opportunity of adding my personal congratulations.'

'Thank you, *Herr Kommodore*.' 'What the hell was this leading up to?' Konrad wondered. Not the Scapa Flow project again surely. After Prien's success the British were certain to have strengthened their defences and no U-boat would stand a cat-in-hell's chance in a future attack.

'How would you like to be a postman, *Kapitanleutnant*?'

Bergman frowned and the movement of his eyebrows sent a sharp pain lancing through his head. He wasn't in the mood for jokes.

'Let me explain straight away that this isn't my idea,' Doenitz said quickly. 'In my view U-boats are built to fight. However . . .' The pause indicated that he was tired of arguing with some petty bureaucrat at the Propaganda Ministry in Berlin. 'During the last war von Arnauld took *U-35* into Cartegena harbour to deliver a personal letter from the Kaiser to the King of Spain. It was regarded as a great propaganda success at the time and von Arnauld received world-wide publicity. I can't imagine why but it just seemed to catch the interest of the world's press. Well, apparently one of Goebbels' whizz-kids at the Ministry thinks we ought to pull a similar stunt this time and they have asked me to provide a U-boat for the purpose. They stipulated that the commander must be well-known and you were suggested along with Prien, Kirchen, and some others. As it happens you are the only one available.'

'What does it involve, sir?' Bergman was intrigued despite himself.

'You are to take a personal letter from the Fuehrer to the President of Mexico, remain in Central American waters for a few days, and then return to Germany. A simple operation, you see.'

'But *UB-44* can't carry enough fuel for a round trip to Mexico and back, sir.'

'I see you don't know your history very well, Bergman. Hans Rose said much the same sort of thing when he was told to patrol off the American coast with *U-53* in 1916. But they managed to find places to store extra fuel and he made it comfortably. Of course,' Doenitz added casually, 'it will mean carrying only half your normal complement of torpedoes - there'll be no room for re-loads. But as it will be a peaceful mission I don't think you need worry on that account. And, in any case, the rest will do you good.'

In other words, thought Konrad, consider yourself under orders. He didn't relish the thought of sailing with only half his torpedoes but the *Kommodore* was right about one thing – the rest would do him good. And the hot Carribean sun would help to soothe away the bitterness that still rankled in his heart.

'You will have to leave on the 17th so I'm afraid you and your men will be celebrating Christmas at sea. *Korvetten-kapitan* von Deusse will be responsible for preparing *UB-44* and the Fuehrer's letter will be delivered to you shortly before you sail. Any questions?'

'No, *Herr Kommodore.*'

'Then it only remains for me to wish you good luck.' Doenitz stood up and grasped Konrad's hand firmly. 'Unfortunately I won't be able to see you off. I have to fly to Berlin this evening. But I will be thinking of you.'

Bergman's heels came together and he bowed stiffly. Then, raising his right hand in the salute he was coming to hate, he turned about and left the Kommodore's office.

That evening, seated in a comfortable armchair in the *Kommando* Room, he listened to the first excited reports of a naval battle in the South Atlantic. According to Berlin Radio the pocket-battleship *Graf Spee,* meeting up with a group of British cruisers, had won a glorious victory. Later reports stated that she was heading for Montevideo to repair superficial battle damage.

Bergman frowned as he reached forward to switch off the radio. There was something odd about the news. Surely if Langsdorff's ship had only received minor damage he would have repaired the *Graf Spee* at sea using his own resources. By entering harbour he was giving up his greatest asset — his ability to vanish into the vast wastes of the ocean. Once in port, even a friendly port, the whole world would know where he was. And the Royal Navy would lose no time in bottling him up inside with an overwhelming force. No, he decided, whatever Berlin might say, *Graf Spee* must be seriously damaged.

Collecting his hat and coat from the orderly on duty in the cloakroom, Bergman hurried back to the dockyard. *UB-44* was still tied up to her old berth at Pier G although most of the crew were either ashore sleeping in barracks or on leave. There was only a care and maintenance party on board and, despite the rota he had drawn up, he was not surprised to find Herzog in charge. There were times when he felt sure that the old veteran didn't have a home — it seemed quite impossible to prise him away from his beloved U-boat.

Bergman entered through the lower conning-tower hatch and closed the black-out curtain before going through into the brightly lit control room. Heinrich, *UB-44*'s senior cook, popped his head out of the galley to see who it was, straightened up as he recognized the captain, and saluted.

'Wasn't expecting you back on board tonight, sir. Shall I wake up the cox'n?'

'No need for that, son,' Herzog boomed as he emerged through the forward bulkhead door. 'Don't you know I *never* sleep!' He welcomed Bergman with an informally friendly salute that would have earned him 7 days loss of privileges on one of the big battle-wagons. 'Can I get you a mug of cocoa, sir?'

'No thank you, Chief. I'm going along to my cabin. See that I am not disturbed.'

Bergman ducked through the control-room hatch and slipped through the curtains into the darkened wardroom. Switching on the light he reached for the small Dutch KB portable that the officers used for off-duty entertainment. As he did so, Konrad glanced anxiously over his shoulder. It reminded him of the occasions when he raided the kitchen at his Munich prep school. And he felt equally guilty.

Sitting down at the table he switched the radio on and began twisting the tuning knob. He remembered his patriotic horror on board *UB-16* when Stohr had listened to the BBC news broadcast at the time of the Munich crisis. Yet now, in a similar situation, he was about to do precisely the same. What was it that Stohr had said; listening to enemy radio broadcasts was an approved means of intelligence. Somehow he doubted whether the High Command would sanction this particular piece of eavesdropping.

He found the wavelength and settled down to listen. The news from London confirmed his worst fears. *Graf Spee* had been caught by the cruisers *Exeter*, *Ajax* and *Achilles*. A running fight had ensued in which *Exeter*, the heaviest of the three cruisers, had suffered serious damage. But, incredibly, *Graf Spee* had broken off the action and entered Montevideo harbour leaving the British warships patrolling off the entrance to the River Plate, like cats waiting to pounce on a mouse sheltering in its hole.

Langsdorff had certainly got himself into a corner, Bergman decided. And the ominous report that 'heavy units of the Royal Navy were now closing in on the area' did little to relieve his anxieties. Perhaps Langsdorff was lying doggo in the knowledge that von Mikel and *Koenig* were on their way. It would need a *very* substantial force to destroy *two* pocket-battleships operating in company. But he was forced to admit that this was only wishful thinking. *Koenig* was quite definitely operating in the North Atlantic and the possibility of a three thousand mile dash to the south was extremely remote. In fact, if von Mikel had any sense, he would take advantage of the British ships steaming hard for the River Plate and attack the trade routes while they were denuded of protective forces.

He switched off the radio. Langsdorff would have to sort out his own problems. Right now, *UB-44*'s projected trip to Mexico had given him more than enough things to think about without worrying over *Graf Spee*'s predicament. Picking up a sheaf of papers he started going over the figures of their probable fuel consumption for the third time.

The morning of 17 December began with a blizzard that quickly shrouded the dockyard with a thick carpet of snow. Winter had started early and the bitter winds sweeping in from Russia promised a bleak future. Bergman looked at the snow and the leaden skies and wished he was at home in Bavaria. The skiing on the Grunnenburg should be superb this Christmas and, if the sun managed to break through, the long sweeping runs would be a fairyland of sparkling whiteness as they swooped down to the huddled houses of Vintenschloss nestling snugly in the shadow of the great mountain. Perhaps next year, when the war was over, he would be able to enjoy it all again.

He trudged back from the Flotilla Commander's office with his lapels turned up against the wind and his head bent forward to minimize the unpleasantness of the driving wet snow. Turning the corner by Barrack Block 15 a blast of wind, tunnelled into compressed fury as it ripped between the tall dockyard buildings, hit him with a force that nearly blew him off his feet. He knocked the caked snow from his greatcoat and swore as he stumbled into a drift that squelched wetly into his shoes. Perhaps Doenitz had been right. With winter coming the hot Carribean sun had distinct attractions.

UB-44 was still firmly secured against Pier G and the telephone landlines and electric cables, feeding current direct from the dockyard's own generators, were festooned with icicles as the water dripping from them froze in the 20-below temperatures.

Doppelheim looked up from the temporary telephone installed on a spare corner of the chart table as Bergman slipped off his snow-caked greatcoat.

'A call for you, sir. Personal.'

What now? Konrad sighed as he took the instrument in his hand. If Walther or von Deusse wanted him back at the Flotilla Office again in this weather he was half a mind to tell them to get stuffed.

'*Kapitanleutnant* Bergman speaking.'

He recognized her voice immediately she spoke.

'I am sorry I was so rude – but it was not as you thought.' Konrad felt his pulse quicken. So she had obviously received the letter he had written on his return from Kiel. 'Before I knew who you really were it didn't matter. But now it is different.'

'I thought I made it clear in my letter that it *isn't* different. I haven't changed.'

'Please God you won't. But things at home are bad. It is not good that an important officer like you should get involved. Remember I am what I am.'

Konrad knew what she was getting at. The anti-semitic element in the Government was getting more influential every day. And he knew, also, that she was picking her words carefully in case the Gestapo were tapping the line. It was getting as bad as that.

'Let me see you,' he urged. 'Just for a few minutes, please.'

'No – for your sake it must finish. Perhaps when all this is over it will be possible. But until then we must wait. Goodbye, my love.'

The telephone clicked and the line went dead. Bergman stood holding the handset to his ear for several seconds before he realized that she had gone. His bitterness vanished only to be replaced by an ache that was infinitely worse to endure. He put the phone down.

'Wipe that silly grin off your face, Cox'n,' he snapped. 'We sail in six hours and I want all stores rechecked.'

Herzog stiffened to attention, saluted, and went aft to supervise the men loading the boxes and cans of food as they were lowered through the after hatch. He felt no resentment at the skipper's uncharacteristic abruptness,. The next operation – whatever it might be – was obviously playing on Bergman's nerves. And he guessed, too, that the Old Man was having trouble with his love life. He shrugged. Give him time to work it out of his system and he'll be okay again.

Bergman was discussing the final details of *UB-44*'s trim and the effect of the extra fuel and stores with Bauer and Engineer Korman when Meister, the Telegraphist, hurried in from the radio room. His face was ashen. He stood to attention and waited. Bergman looked up.

'Yes, Meister?'

'It's the *Graf Spee,* sir.' His voice was trembling. 'I've just heard a special announcement on Berlin Radio. She's been scuttled, sir.'

'Thank you, Meister.' Bergman thought quickly. This was hardly the best time for morale to be undermined. 'Pass the news to the crew over the loudspeakers. Tell them that the Fuehrer, realizing that *Graf Spee* faced certain destruction if she sailed out against the overwhelming enemy forces that had gathered off Montevideo, decided to scuttle her to save the lives of her crew.' He paused in search of more lies. 'Tell them that the Fuehrer sends no German sailor to his death in a useless cause.'

Quite the proper little Nazi, thought Bauer as he listened. He hoped he would never have cause to give out such a load of crap when *he* got command of a U-boat.

146

Leaving their thoughts unspoken the three officers returned to their discussion of the alterations required in the ballast loading to maintain trim. There was no room for personal feelings or animosities when it came to *UB-44*'s safety. At the moment she was their snugly comfortable home – a haven of warmth in the freezing snowstorms that were sweeping across northern Germany. But she could just as easily become their tomb. And they knew it.

The Mercedes staff car sloshed through the soft snow and slid to a halt at the entrance to Pier G. Already warned of its imminent arrival by a telephone call from the Main Gate, Bergman was up on the jetty waiting. A *Feldwebel* stepped out of the front right-hand door, ran quickly round the back of the vehicle and opened the rear door on the opposite side and nearest to where *UB-44*'s captain was standing. A highly polished jack-boot emerged and sank to its pristine ankle in the snow.

Oberstleutnant Manfred von Hoppner, Special Equerry to the Fuehrer, was an imposing figure. His smartly tailored uniform looked as if it had come straight from the window of a military outfitters and the deep red lining of his field-cape was in sharp contrast to the sombre whiteness of the snow. He held a small despatch box in an immaculately gloved hand.

Bergman saluted – the effect being slightly marred by the miniature avalanche of snow that cascaded from his sleeve as he raised his arm. Von Hoppner returned the compliment and motioned the U-boat captain to one side where they could not be overheard by the sentries. He seemed unconcerned by the biting cold and stood with his cape flapping open.

'*Konteradmiral* Doenitz* has already given you details of your mission so I need not elaborate. This is the box containing the letter. It is to be handed over personally to the

*Karl Doenitz was promoted to the rank of Rear Admiral in October, 1939.

147

Reich Ambassador on your arrival. He will have arranged full press coverage so make sure you are wearing your best uniform, dear boy.' He looked at Bergman's workstained face with a delicate shudder. 'And for goodness sake have a shave before you go ashore.'

Why doesn't someone tell him there's a war on, thought Bergman. These bloody poofs from OKW* were more concerned with their wardrobes than with the war. Strutting ossified peacocks!

Aloud he said, 'Of course, *Herr Oberstleutnant.*'

Von Hoppner handed him the despatch box. 'The Fuehrer wishes me to inform you that he sends you and the men under your command his personal good wishes for the success of your mission.'

'Big deal,' thought Bergman. 'I'd rather he'd sent me a full outfit of torpedoes and given me a free hand to use them on the right targets.'

'So good luck, *Kapitanleutnant*. Heil Hitler!'

UB-44's skipper raised his right hand obediently but the Special Equerry was already back inside the snugness of his heated limousine. The straight-eight engine came to life and the rear wheels spat muddy slush over Bergman's trousers as they spun in the snow. He watched the big Mercedes drive back towards the Main Gates, shrugged, and turned back to the U-boat. What a reward for sinking a British cruiser – running errands and delivering letters for Adolf! And listening to some pansy from headquarters telling him what he should wear and when he should shave. God almighty! What *was* Germany coming to?

At 1900 hours precisely, with the despatch box locked securely inside the wardroom safe, *UB-44* slipped out of Wilhelmshaven on the flood tide. The blizzard was still raging and it was difficult to see more than a hundred yards ahead but Bergman handled the submarine with the easy

*Oberkommando of the Wermacht – the supreme command organization of all three German fighting services.

confidence of the veteran he had become. Six men were stationed on the fore deck and a further four aft of the conning-tower. Each man was equipped with a steel boathook and their task was to keep the main vents clear of ice in case it proved necessary to order an emergency dive. Two more seamen chipped at the frozen snow rimming the conning-tower hatch while a third, his breath turning to ice on his beard, wiped the periscope lens continuously with a cloth soaked in methylated spirits.

Despite his two sweaters and heavy leather topcoat Bergman shivered as *UB-44* felt her way through the darkness. He wondered how the men would react when they learned they were en route for the Carribean. His alert eyes picked out the dark shape of the picket-boat patrolling the outer defence line.

'Slow ahead both. 'midships helm.'

Deep down in the snug warmth of the U-boat's belly he heard the sharp ting of the engine-room telegraph and the helmsman's robot repetition of his orders.

' 'midships, sir.'

A shaded white light punctuated the darkness with a series of long and short flashes as the armed trawler made the routine challenge.

'*What Ship*?'

'Stream the lights, Kibbert.'

The shaded blue and white lamps clamped to the stays of the periscope standard, carefully set in a pre-arranged pattern that was altered for every new patrol, blinked to life. Bergman counted off ten seconds exactly.

'Kill the lights!'

The lamps cut off like the candles on a birthday cake being blown out. But they had remained alight long enough for the keen-eyed skipper of the picket-boat.

'Blue – blue – white – blue – white.'

Dortmund's mate scanned the daily list of recognition signals and nodded.

'*UB-44*, Georg. Shall I send the clearance signal?'

'Aye, go ahead. She was due through the outer defence line at 1925 so she's a minute early.' Despite his own years of experience as a deep-sea fisherman there was a grudging note of admiration in his voice. 'How the hell they can keep to time in this weather beats me. But then, if you ask me, these U-boat skippers are more like bloody fish than men!'

The crisp dot-dash of the letter 'A' repeated continuously for ten seconds told Bergman he had been recognized and he passed through the boom defences. Somewhere in the distance ahead an old donkey-engine shuddered to life and, although she was invisible in the driving snow, the gate vessel swung the heavy boom aside – the rasp of its wire cables sliding through the frozen pulleys sounding like the shrill screams of Ancient Greece's legendary Sirens luring another ship to its doom. Bergman, fortunately, had insufficient imagination to see the connection. To his practical ear it meant one thing – the boom gate was open.

'Full ahead both!'

UB-44 gathered speed and headed for the narrow gap. All U-boat captains regarded it as a point of honour to clear the boom at maximum revolutions whether it was visible or not. And the present weather conditions only added to the challenge. With Bauer looking to the port side Bergman stared ahead to starboard searching for a glimpse of the gate vessel's navigation lights. Suddenly, almost dead ahead, a red lamp appeared.

'Port 5!'

The U-boat heeled slightly under the helm and the red light moved smoothly to the right as the submarine's bows swung towards the gate.

'Midships!'

He could now see the green light on the other gate vessel gleaming faintly through the driving wall of snow. Just a touch of the helm and they were through.

'Starboard 5 . . . steady as she goes . . . 'midships!'

The boom lights were extinguished as quickly as they appeared and *UB-44* found herself alone on a black sea, her bows dipping into the long swell of the Bight, and then rising again as if to throw off the freezing water flooded down her fo'c'sle before it could glaze into ice. The sea kept the prow clear of snow but the deck party, clinging to the safety line as the submarine pitched and tumbled in the darkness, had to work like beavers to keep the rest of the hull clear.

Bergman had had enough. He knew that he should remain on the surface to take advantage of his powerful diesel engines but the heavy icing was increasing *UB-44*'s top-weight alarmingly and the sharp rolling motion made him worry about stability. There was only one safe place in this weather. And that was deep down under the surface of the sea where the warmer water would quickly melt the ice. That it also meant a means of escape from the freezing hell of watch-keeping on the exposed bridge did not pass unnoticed.

'Stand by to dive. Clear the bridge. Deck party below.'

As the last of the lookouts squeezed through the upper hatch Bergman found himself alone with Bauer on the empty bridge. The blizzard had died away and the snowflakes were falling gently as they used to when he watched them through the nursery window. The world was still and dark and, as the clouds began to break, the first twinkling stars peeped down. *UB-44* looked like a slender iced cake floating on a sea of black velvet and the war suddenly seemed a million miles away.

Reaching forward, Bergman scooped a handful of snow from the flat steel ledge of the conning-tower, crumpled it into a hard ball of ice, and threw it at his First Lieutenant. Bauer dodged the missile with a laugh, grabbed some snow for himself and retaliated. For the next few minutes the two officers threw off their responsibilities and relived their carefree youth in a cheerful breathless snowball fight. Bergman was still laughing as he dragged the upper hatch cover shut

and fastened the clips before following Bauer down into the
control room.

Three weeks and 6,000 nautical miles later *UB-44* made
her appointed rendezvous with a disguised German tanker
for refuelling. They were down to less than ten tons of oil
and the U-boat sucked greedily at the umbilical hose to
re-fill her empty bunkers. The oil barrels stored in the forward torpedo compartment gave Bergman a further range
of 1,000 miles at optimum cruising speed but, from now on,
he would have to watch fuel consumption with a miserly eye.

With two days left before their scheduled arrival at
Tampico, on the eastern coast of Mexico, Bergman decided
to paint ship. Finding a small uninhabited island they
anchored close inshore and set to work.

It was reasonably safe. The British Navy had no cause
to suspect that a U-boat was operating deep inside the Gulf
of Mexico and the United States Navy was still neutral.
Their chances of being spotted were remote but Bergman
retained his old cautious instinct for survival. Lookouts were
posted and the anti-aircraft crew sat alongside the 20mm
gun playing cards in the sun – instantly ready to man their
weapon at the first alarm.

By evening *UB-44* was shining like a new toy. The matt
war paint that had dulled her metalwork to render her less
conspicuous had been patiently chipped away and the brass
gleamed and sparkled in the sunlight. Bergman looked down
from his vantage point on the bridge and felt an understand-
able pride in the U-boat's immaculate appearance.

'Starboard Watch – all hands to bathe!'

It was almost too good to be true and the men, their pale
faces now tanned brown by the tropical sun, hesitated for
a moment when they heard the unexpected order. Then
someone dived into the warm green water and the surface
churned to white froth as the rest followed suit.

Bergman allowed them thirty minutes. Then he called

them back on deck, gave them fifteen minutes to dry off and dress, and then told them to take over the Duty Watch so that their comrades could share the fun. The sun, a smooth ball of red fire, was sinking slowly down below the horizon as the last man clambered back on board.

U-44's diesels roared to life and the submarine swung away from the island for the last 180 miles of her mail run. At midnight, as the men gathered for their main meal, Bergman explained the purpose of their long voyage to the south-west, and warned them to wear No 1 rig for the forenoon watch.

'We are due at Tampico at 1000 hours. I intend to approach the coast submerged and to surface at two bells. The intention is to make our arrival as dramatic as possible. Every man of the off-duty watch will proceed on deck and dress ship as we enter the harbour. And remember this. We are Germany's ambassadors and the eyes and ears of the world will be upon us. I regret that I cannot authorize shore leave but you will all understand that we must be at instant readiness to leave should the Royal Navy decide to send in a reception committee.

'Finally, although the reporters and cameramen will not be allowed on board they will undoubtedly come alongside to obtain interviews and pictures. I want you to be polite and courteous to them at all times but, and I stress this, you must on no account answer their questions. That is all. Stand down to dinner.'

CHAPTER NINE

Conference Room One was already occupied by Goering and members of his senior *Luftwaffe* staff. Conference Room Two was being redecorated. So Grand Admiral Raeder and the *Kriegsmarine's* top brass were accommodated in Conference Room Three – a small bare-walled concrete bunker some distance from the main command complex of the *Wolfsschanze*.* It was inadequately heated and poorly lit., But, so far as Adolf Hitler was concerned, anything was good enough for the Navy. The *Kriegsmarine* was not his favourite branch of the *Wehrmacht*.

The Fuehrer entered the bunker at 1027 precisely. The fact that the meeting had been called for 0900 hours was not overlooked by the Naval Staff but they had long since grown accustomed to such snubs. Throwing himself into an armchair at the head of the table he wasted no time on preliminaries and his voice was heavy with sarcasm.

'Tell me, Herr Grand Admiral, it has often puzzled me. Why do we bother to have a Navy?'

Raeder, stung by the question, took the bait and launched into his often-repeated defence of the *Kriegsmarine* – its role in Germany's war strategy, the theory of the 'fleet in being', the necessity of crippling Britain's seaborne trade routes. His speech, a model resumé of naval strategic theory eminently suited as a lecture at a staff college seminar, was listened to with growing impatience by Hitler.

'. . . and to conclude, my Fuehrer, if Germany did not possess a Navy our most dangerous enemy, Great Britain, would be in a position to win the war tomorrow.'

'Then tell me, *Herr Grossadmiral,* if we have such a fine

*Hitler's 'wolf's lair' near Rastenburg in East Prussia.

efficient navy why is it our ships that get sunk and not those of the enemy?'

'With respect, my Fuehrer, it is the enemy who are losing ships not us. The battleship *Royal Oak,* the carrier *Courageous* . . .' he took a slip of paper passed to him by one of the Staff and glanced down to refresh his memory. '. . . the destroyers *Blanche* and *Gipsy* . . .'

Hitler held up a hand to stop him.

'I am not unaware of enemy losses, my dear Raeder. But, pray enlighten me, how were they sunk?'

'Either by mines or U-boats, Fuehrer.'

'Precisely,' Hitler said triumphantly. 'Do you realize that for the cost of a single battleship I could build five squadrons of bombers. I sometimes wonder why I allowed you to squander Germany's money on your useless big ships when they seem to spend most of their time skulking in harbours.'

Raeder sighed. 'I am sorry, Fuehrer, but your facts are incorrect – our battle fleet is playing a vital part in the war. A "fleet in being" ties down the enemy's naval forces. And you seem to have forgotten our ocean raiders – the *Graf Spee* . . .'

Hitler's fist smashed down on the table with a force that upset one of the glass drinking jugs. 'I have *not* forgotten the *Graf Spee, Herr Grossadmiral.* It remains very fresh in my mind. And what happened? *I* had to order it to be scuttled to save the honour of the Third Reich!'

The *Oberkommando Kriegsmarine* remained silent. *Graf Spee* had done a good job within the limitations of the naval situation. And she would have gone down with colours flying if Hitler had not issued his infamous order. The indignity had been so great that Langsdorff, her captain, had committed suicide rather than face the dishonour Berlin had forced upon him.

'And this morning,' Hitler continued, 'I learn from Goering that the *Koenig* is in a similar situation. Badly

155

damaged by two British cruisers and running for her life to the sanctuary of a neutral port.'

'Von Mikel fought well against superior forces, *mein Fuehrer*. He sank the British cruiser *Coronel* before his ship was crippled.'

'I should hope so. If my memory serves me correctly *Koenig* mounts 11-inch guns while the *Coronel* carried only 6-inch weapons. The issue should have been beyond doubt as soon as they came within range.'

Raeder sighed again. It was impossible to make Hitler understand the problems of sea warfare – he judged everything by paper statistics or military standards. The fact that von Mikel was fighting 5,000 miles from his home base while the British were only a few hundred miles from their West Indies' harbours seemed beyond his comprehension. But he had learned that when the Fuehrer was in one of his rages it was better to let him rant on until he lost interest in the subject and stormed out of the room.

'What is the latest news, Raeder? I have the impression that naval signals pass direct to OKM before being reported to OKW. I suppose,' he added with heavy sarcasm, 'this is so you can censor them first.'

The Grand Admiral ignored the insult.

'A report was received at 0845 this morning that *Koenig* has anchored in a small Mexican harbour – Puerto Laros – and has requested permission to remain for seventy-two hours to carry out repairs.'

Hitler's face darkened with anger. He stood up suddenly, his entire body shaking with rage. 'So it is to be the *Graf Spee* all over again. Does the honour of the Third Reich – *my* honour, *Grossadmiral* – mean nothing to you.'

'I would not recommend scuttling,' Raeder said tentatively.

'You will recommend nothing, do you hear, *nothing*! Report to my War Room at 1800 hours this evening. *I* will decide what happens to *my* ships.'

Followed by his train of sychophantic advisers Hitler stormed out of Conference Room Three leaving the Navy Staff to ponder the scarcely veiled threat contained in his final words. Raeder was the first to recover from the shock.

'Something must be done, gentlemen. I have few illusions regarding the Fuehrer's ultimate decision.'

'We can't use radio communication,' von Schroeder pointed out. 'An enemy shell has completely wiped out *Koenig's* wireless office. It would be impossible to replace the equipment except at one of our home bases. Von Mikel could rig an emergency transmitter – the *Type TZ-50* all our ships carry in reserve – but with a maximum range of only fifty miles it would be useless.'

'Where is the nearest German Consulate to Puento Laros?' asked Raeder.

'I think it would be Count Manstein at Tampico. I'd have to check when we returned to HQ. But there are coding problems and we daren't send signals *en clair*. In addition Tampico must be nearly two hundred miles to the south and *Koenig's* emergency receiver would not have the power to transmit a reply.'

The Grand Admiral was thinking. Despite his remoteness from day-to-day operations he normally knew and remembered all major fleet dispositions. He began to smile.

'There is a U-Boat at Tampico at the moment – on some damn fool mission dreamed up by Goebbels. Her captain will have the code books on board and she can move closer to *Koenig* to act as radio link. And if von Mikel's cypher books have been destroyed the U-Boat can decode as necessary.' He paused to consider the details. 'If we send a code signal to the Embassy in Mexico City they can repeat it to their Consul in Tampico who will pass it to the U-Boat. Once communications are established the Embassy can radio direct to the U-Boat who can then re-transmit to *Koenig*. Von Mikel's *TZ-50* set can be used over a short range to pass a reply to the submarine and it can then be passed back to OKM by the same channels in reverse. Once we have established a direct link to *Koenig* the Fuehrer will have to accept the traditional rule that the man on the spot, von Mikel, knows the local situation best and should be left to act according to his judgement.'

Christian von Schroeder, the Director of Operations, looked doubtful. 'But that's precisely what we told the Fuehrer when Langsdorff took *Graf Spee* into Montevideo. And look what notice he took.'

Raeder stood up. He looked tired. The constant battles with Hitler were more exhausting than fighting the enemy. And considerably less palatable.

'I know, Christian, I know. But we must *try* to do something. Inform me as soon as communications are established.'

The hot Mexican sun was just the tonic Bergman needed after being cooped up in *UB-44* for three weeks. The mail-bag mission, ridiculous as it had seemed when he first heard about it, had proved to be a great propaganda success. The Fuehrer's letter had been handed over to the Ambassador in front of more than fifty whirring newsreel cameras and several hundred pressmen and news of the U-Boat's impudent arrival quickly flashed around the world. He had been especially pleased with the admiring comments made about the smartness of *UB-44* and her crew. In fact some commentators, drawing snap conclusions from inadequate evidence, told their readers and listeners that Nazi Germany was obviously fighting the war without strain and with typical Teutonic efficiency.

Sitting on the Consulate veranda, he sipped a long iced drink and scanned the foreign newspaper reports of his activities, with the perfume of hibiscus scenting the warm air. The atmosphere of peaceful tranquility seemed a million miles away from the grim gloom of Europe's first winter of war and it was already difficult to remember the reality of the blizzards that had been sweeping northern Germany

158

on the evening of their departure. It was a pity they had missed Christmas at home but, with ingenious enthusiasm, *UB-44*'s crew had celebrated the occasion despite the unseasonal surrounds in which they lived. Herzog, with the experience of many previous Christmases at sea, built an intricate fir tree from paper and card which, duly decorated, was placed in a central position in the forward crew's space. Chief Cook Heinrich made the best of their canned meats and, by some logistical miracle inspired by the coxswain, had contrived to smuggle a number of small Xmas puddings on board before they sailed.

Like all U-boats *UB-44* was 'dry' and toasts had to be drunk in lime juice but not even this detracted from the spirit of gaiety and bonhomie that embraced the crew in its warm friendly arms. Bergman had made a short speech and the toast was 'The Fatherland and Victory'. Then two of the engine-room mechanics produced mouth-organs and the strains of carols echoed through the steel vault of the U-boat floating deep below the surface of the ocean.

Bergman's sleepy memories stopped abruptly as he turned the pages of *The New York Herald Tribune* and saw the 'Stop Press'.

ATLANTIC SEA BATTLE

German commerce raider in battle with British warships. One cruiser reported sunk. Heavy damage to Nazi ship. Unconfirmed report that raider was pocket-battleship *Koenig.* (AP & Reuters).

Konrad was wide awake now. Glancing at the date of the newspaper he ferreted through the pile lying on top of the bamboo table at his side. He found the following day's *Tribune.* By now the story had broken to a front page lead. He read :

The British Admiralty revealed last night that cruisers of the West Indies Squadron encountered the pocket-battleship *Koenig* while it was sinking the French tanker *D'Auberville* in the Gulf of Mexico. A fierce battle followed during which the German raider was seriously damaged. It was last seen fleeing on a south-westerly course heavily on fire and under cover of a smoke-screen. The official British communique admits the loss of the old cruiser *Coronel*, a veteran of World War I, and damage, described as superficial, to two other warships. There has so far been no report of the battle from Berlin Radio or official German sources.

Bergman had never liked von Mikel but he was always the first to admit that *Koenig*'s captain was a fighter of the old school. A gunnery lieutenant with Hipper's First Scouting Group at Jutland in 1916, he had won the Iron Cross (1st Class) when his battle-cruiser took part in the famous 'Death Ride'. And he had been a prominent ringleader in the plan to scuttle the surrendered German Fleet in Scapa Flow after the Armistice. If von Mikel turned tail and fled the field of battle it could only mean one thing – *Koenig* was very seriously damaged. And that meant the possibility of the *Graf Spee* disgrace all over again.

Yet von Mikel was no Langsdorff – Bergman was quite certain on that score. If his ship had to go to the bottom it would be with colours flying in the face of the enemy. *Kapitan zur See* Ernst Fredrich von Mikel was not a man to scuttle his command to preserve the Fuehrer's honour even when disobedience meant certain death. But what the hell could he do with a crippled ship 5,000 miles from his nearest home base.

Bergman looked up as a shadow passed across the veranda. The Consul, Count Manstein, was standing by his chair holding a teleprinter message.

'I have just received this cypher message from the Embassy, *Kapitanleutnant*. It is marked for your attention – Most Immediate.'

Konrad stood up and took the slip of paper. He recognized the coded opening. It was the cypher used for confidential signals to a commander afloat – the restricted KK code which could not be put through the standard cypher machine for decoding. And he recognized the code name of the signal's originator. It was from Raeder himself!

'I must get back to the *UB-44* immediately, sir. This is a matter of exceptional urgency. If a further signal is received from the Ambassador please have it brought to the harbour without delay.'

After twenty years of service in the soporific sunshine of Mexico the Count was unused to such bustle – there was always tomorrow. But he was astute enough to realize from the *Kapitanleutnant's* expression that something important was in the wind. Instinctively his back stiffened with long-forgotten discipline as memories of his days as a staff officer on the Western Front returned. And the unexpected excitement brought a new sparkle to his tired watery eyes.

'Of course, Kapitanleutnant.'

'Why the teleprinter?' Bergman asked as he found his cap and made for the door. 'Surely radio would be quicker.'

'The Embassy has no wireless links with its Consulates – our normal activities are usually commercial rather than military. A teleprinter channel is quite adequate.'

The U-boat captain nodded. 'I suppose you're right. I shall probably need to communicate direct with the Embassy when I've decoded the signal. Call them up on the teleprinter and get their wavelength. I'll wait in the harbour until you can telephone it to me – they've run a temporary land-line out to our mooring buoy.'

'Of course, *Kapitanleutnant*. I will do so immediately.'

But Bergman had already climbed into the Consulate's antiquated Austro-Daimler and was being driven out of the gates.

The newsmen clustered around the moored U-Boat in their hired launches received brusque acknowledgement from Konrad as the Harbourmaster's day-boat brought him alongside. Essen had quickly mustered a deck party to pipe the captain aboard with due ceremony as he saw the boat

161

approaching but *UB-44*'s commander hurried past without even returning the salute. Christ, thought Essen, what the hell's happened now?

Bauer was waiting at the foot of the ladder as Bergman came down into the control room. There was an expression on the captain's face that boded no questions.

'Clear the wardroom, Number One. And put a guard outside to prevent anyone entering. Then prepare to cast off in fifteen minutes.' Bauer went aft to execute the orders while Bergman ducked into the pint-sized wireless cabin.

'The *Koenig* is at Puento Laros,' he told Meister. 'That's about forty miles north east from here. Her radio is out of action and she is probably using an emergency *TZ-50* portable transmitter. Get into contact and tell them we are acting as radio link with Berlin. Use the standard January code. When you have established communications inform them to stand-by for a KK cypher message. Have you got all that?'

'Yes sir.'

'Good – get cracking.'

Leading Seaman Zeiten was already on guard outside the wardroom curtain with an official issue Walther P-38 pistol holstered snugly at his waist. Bergman closed the curtain behind him, drew the teleprinter message from his inside pocket, and opened the safe. The KK Code was in a small blue-bound book weighted with lead along its spine to ensure that it would sink to the bottom in an emergency. He put it down on the table alongside the OKM signal and got to work.

As the cypher gradually revealed its secrets he was torn between disappointment at its apparently mundane contents and excitement at its hidden implications. When he had finished decoding he sat back and read it.

Most Immediate. OKM to Commander UB-44. Top Secret.

Proceed to sea all speed. Action preparedness immediate. Contact von Mikel in KK code and pass my signal. Trans-

162

mit reply KK code to OKM via Ambassador Kolnburg. Priority all stages. Raeder.

Onward transmission signal: OKM to Commander HK-23. Report details damage sustained, repair prospects, enemy situation, and proposed action. Essential immediate reply via UB-44. KK code all stages. Raeder.

Bergman picked up the coded version of the signal and took it across to the wireless room. Meister, earphones clamped to his head, was scribbling rapidly.

'I'm in contact with *Koenig,* sir. They're using a *TZ-50* transmitter but the power's low and I'm only picking her up at Strength 2. They're standing by.'

'Right, get this off to *Koenig* immediately,' Bergman told him as he handed over the bottom half of the teleprinter message. 'And prefix it KK.'

Meister's right hand rested delicately on the transmitting key as he began tapping the signal. The jumble of letters and figures meant nothing to him and he worked like an automaton.

'Telephone for you, sir.'

Konrad nodded and hurried into the control room and picked up the phone. It was Manstein. He wrote the wavelength on a piece of paper and put the receiver down.

'Are we nearly ready to cast off, Number One?'

'Yes, sir.'

'Good – get the telephone line disconnected and advise the Harbourmaster we will be leaving within the next hour. I'll let you know when.'

He went back into the radio office. The waiting was the worst part. But of course von Mikel would have to decode the signal personally, as he had done, and then encode his reply before answering. It would all take time. And the top brass in Berlin were probably sweating more than he was. It would be bloody awkward if *Koenig's* books had been destroyed in the battle. But fortunately they were safe and, as he stood there waiting, Meister began taking down von

163

Mikel's reply. He asked for a repeat of one group, then tapped out his acknowledgement and handed the signal pad to the captain.

Back inside the wardroom Bergman opened the KK code book again and started to check the accuracy of the message. Better to ask for a repetition at this stage than to transmit errors back to OKM. It was an unauthorised procedure but it seemed sensible.

Von Mitel, CO HK-23, to OKM via UB-44
Turret Anton destroyed. Only three 11-in. guns operating. Half starboard secondary armament out of action. Spotting aircraft burned out. Main transmitter destroyed. No damage below waterline. Maximum speed 20 knots. 108 killed 69 wounded. Ammunition down to 30%. Two enemy cruisers patrolling off three mile limit. Local intelligence reports heavy units closing in. Propose to fight clear before enemy reinforced. Minimum repairs maximum time twelve hours. Von Mikel.

Bergman whistled softly as he read the message. *Koenig* was in a bad way. If the British caught her she wouldn't stand a chance. But it was typical of von Mikel to risk all in open battle and damn the odds! Obviously OKM intended to make use of *UB-44* somewhere along the line – the question was *how*? Surely they weren't intending to just keep the U-boat as an emergency radio link. Konrad began to picture the situation in his mind. The only possibility he could envisage was a torpedo attack on the British cruisers just as the pocket-battleship put to sea. Von Mikel might just slip through the cordon in the ensuing confusion. And if *UB-44* should be lucky enough to sink one of the cruisers then *Koenig* stood an odds-on chance of breaking clear.

Picking up the slips of paper on which he had decoded the messages Bergman crumpled them into a ball, dropped them into an ashtray and set light to them. He could not take chances on anyone reading the secret KK signals. He went through to the radio room and gave Meister the cypher groups that made up von Mikel's reply together with the Embassy's wavelength. The Telegraphist nodded and turned the dials as he began transmitting *UB-44*'s automatic call-sign. His face was a study in grim concentration as he searched the ether for an acknowledgement. Konrad patted him on the back encouragingly and went back to the control room.

'Cast off, Number One. Steer south down the coast as soon as we clear the buoyed channel and don't turn north until we are out of sight of land – the enemy is sure to have coast-watchers spying on us. If the pressmen try to follow us in their boats – or in an aircraft – dive to 100 feet as soon as we are out of territorial waters and delay the change of course until we are submerged.'

As Bauer shinned up the ladder to the bridge to take *UB-44* out of the harbour Bergman walked across to the chart table where Hauptmann was busy laying out the plot. He leaned over the table and dropped his voice to a sharp whisper.

'Once we have turned north I want you to give Bauer a track for Puento Laros. Find me a spot about six miles to the south of the bay where I will be in a suitable position to receive and transmit signals but where I can also work into a good attacking position on the British squadron.'

'Where are they, sir?'

'Your guess is as good as mine, pilot. But they'll be trying to cover *Koenig*'s probable escape route. You give me an estimated position and I'll back it to my last pfennig.'

UB-44's diesels burst into life with a shuddering roar and Bergman felt the submarine start to move as Bauer steered her out of Tampico harbour. He went back into the ward-room and sat down. He felt suddenly tired. The brief inter-lude of peace and relaxation was over. The grim grey menace of war had descended again and, with it, all the hatred and frustration he felt for what he represented.

Strange that he always experienced these moods of depression before going into action. He had anticipated a surging elation of excitement as his nerves tautened to fever pitch in readiness for danger. But instead he felt only a nagging fear that it was all pointless – that life held something deeper and more important for him than exercising the skilful art of underwater killing. Closing his eyes for a few moments he began to think about Rahel Yousoff.

The faces of Raeder's 'inner circle' of senior staff officers grew progressively grimmer as Hebermund, the Admiral's Flag Lieutenant, read out von Mikel's signal. The situation was more desperate than even their most pessimistic forecasts and there was a studied reluctance to answer when the *Grossadmiral* asked :

'Well, gentlemen, what do we do?'

Shelve all responsibility and put the burden of decision on the shoulders of the man on the spot – that would certainly be one way of escaping the consequences of *Koenig*'s hurried flight from disaster. But that was the coward's way out and they knew it. Reinforcements? No, that was impossible too. Von Schroeder, characteristically searching for straws, was the only one to offer practical suggestion.

'*UB-44* is in the area and she's carrying half her outfit of torpedoes. If von Mikel is determined to fight his way out the U-boat could make some form of diversionary attack on the enemy covering force – or even act as a decoy to lure them away.'

Raeder nodded. 'My mind was working along similar lines. I have known *Kapitan* von Mikel for a great number of years and, given the slightest chance, he will fight. And if he chooses to do so it is our duty to help him in every way we can. Are we agreed, gentlemen?'

The staff officers nodded.

The Fuehrer listened carefully as Raeder read out von Mikel's report and outlined his plan to use *UB-44*.

'It is all we can do,' he concluded. 'Von Mikel can fight or he can surrender. There is no other choice.'

'He could still deprive the enemy of victory by scuttling his ship,' Hitler pointed out. 'I have no wish to see *Koenig* sent to the bottom by British guns. And surrender is completely out of the question.'

'But, Fuehrer, *Koenig* has a good chance of escaping if the U-boat creates a diversion. It is a risk worth taking.'

Hitler was losing interest in the discussion. Naval affairs bored him and his patience, not one of his strongest virtues, was fast evaporating.

'You have read the report, *Grossadmiral*. Von Mikel is in command of a cripple. I have reliable information that the British battlecruiser *Hood* and other heavy ships are already patrolling the area.'

'With respect, Fuehrer, I doubt if the reports are true. The British used the same psychological pressure at Montevideo. And it turned out that their nearest capital ship was more than a thousand miles away. In my judgement the enemy has only two old cruisers, both probably damaged, off Puento Laros. If *UB-44* can dispose of one, *Koenig* has an evens chance of getting away.'

The expression on Hitler's face reflected his disdain for Raeder and the rest of the OKM top-brass. He brought the discussion to an abrupt close by informing one of his aides to call Goering in for a conference about the Luftwaffe's latest manpower requirements. Then he turned to Raeder.

'Send a signal to von Mikel. Tell him it is my express order that he is to scuttle *Koenig* by noon tomorrow. And report his acknowledgement to me personally as soon as it is received.'

It proved to be a difficult signal to phrase and it was over an hour before the *Grossadmiral* finally approved the wording. He handed the draft to von Schroeder for transmission.

'I am going to my quarters. I have no intention of fighting battles that are lost before they have even started.' He sighed

167

wearily. 'I will have no further part in this farce and I am not to be disturbed under *any* circumstances. When *Koenig* acknowledges I want you, von Schroeder, to report the signal to the Fuehrer. You have my authority to make any necessary decisions and I will approve whatever steps you take without question. Goodnight, gentlemen.'

The Director of Operations understood Raeder's feeling of frustration. And he felt no resentment at the delegation of authority. He went through into the teleprinter room, waited while Kapitan Ziller encoded the fateful signal into the KK cypher, and then handed it to the Telegraphist sitting at the keyboard. Returning to his private office he sat down at his desk to await von Mikel's reply.

Bergman rechecked the signal carefully when the Embassy repeater station passed it on to *UB-44*. There must be some mistake in the transmission, he thought. Surely Hitler doesn't propose to sacrifice *another* pocket-battleship in a misguided attempt to save the Nazi flag from defeat for the second time. Goebbels might have succeeded in glossing over the unpleasant truth of the *Graf Spee* incident – but he could never pull the same trick twice. And what would von Mikel's reaction be when he read the humiliating order?

He passed the coded groups of words to Meister and told him to transmit them to *Koenig*. Now, like von Schroeder, he could only wait – an impotent messenger running radio errands. He began to plan what *he* could do to support *Koenig*'s captain if von Mikel obeyed the order. There were four 21inch torpedoes in the bow tubes and just sufficient fuel. With luck he might succeed in nobbling one of the cruisers. Or, perhaps, he could swoop into Puento Laros at night and pick up the most important officers and bring them back to Germany. Dismissing the dreams from his mind he returned to the immediate realities of the situation. When the crunch came he knew he would have to obey orders and so would von Mikel. Where would the *Kriegsmarine* be if its senior officers took their own decisions and ignored the commands they received from OKM. It was unthinkable.

'Reply from *Koenig,* sir.'

Meister handed the slip to Bergman and vanished discreetly as *UB-44*'s captain began decoding the groups of letters. Konrad worked quickly and, as he deciphered the code, he began to smile. He could well imagine what effect von Mikel's signal would have on Hitler's blood pressure. Ducking through the curtains he handed the slip to the Telegraphist.

'Transmit to OKM via the Embassy. And stand by for a reply.'

He went back into the wardroom, burned his decoded copy of the signal, and sat back on the settee. He was still smiling.

Von Schroeder's face paled as Ziller gave him the decoded message. It was impossible. But von Mikel had made it crystal clear. Not daring to disturb Raeder, the Director of Operations put on his cap and, accompanied by his two aides, set off down the thickly carpeted corridor to Hitler's War Room. He felt a little like a man about to enter a lion's den.

The Fuehrer took the pink signal slip and put his glasses on to read it.

From CO HK-23 to OKM via UB-44
Your 1647 refers. Scuttling not considered in best interests of the Third Reich. Intend to sail at dawn and engage the enemy. Please instruct UB-44 to support me. Long live the Fuehrer. Von Mikel.

Hitler's hands were trembling with rage as he took off his glasses and put them down on the desk. He pointed a quivering finger at von Schroeder.

'Disobedience of orders is an act of mutiny, *Vizeadmiral.* I want von Mikel placed under close arrest immediately and a successor appointed to take command of *Koenig.*'

'But, Fuehrer, that is impossible.'

'Silence!' Hitler's hands clenched and thumped the desk.

'Are you daring to disobey my orders as well, von Schroeder?
Is the Navy completely incapable of doing *anything* I command.' His mind suddenly went off at a tangent. 'And where is Raeder? I suppose he dare not show his face.'

The Director of Operations had seen the Fuehrer's outbreaks of blind temper before. He decided to stick to his guns and talk him into reason.

'*Koenig* is five thousand miles away. At that distance we cannot enforce orders. And we have no way of implementing your instruction to arrest von Mikel. All signals are being transmitted in KK code. As you know, this code can only be deciphered by the Commanding Officer, so von Mikel would read the order before anyone else saw it. And obviously, in the circumstances, he would ensure that no one else *did* see it.'

Hitler's original outburst of anger was fading but his hands were still twitching.

'How dare he defy me! His mind is clearly unhinged.'

'Precisely, mein Fuehrer,' von Schroeder agreed diplomatically.

'So we cannot expect him to carry out *any* order we send him.' He stood up suddenly and began pacing the room in silence. No one had the courage to speak and the men in the War Room waited anxiously. Hitler stopped pacing, turned quickly and faced von Schroeder. His eyes were blazing with excitement as he saw a solution.

'If von Mikel will not sink the *Koenig* when I order him to do so, I will see that it is sunk for him!'

He patted the Director of Operations on the shoulder and started to laugh.

'But how, Fuehrer?' Von Schroeder asked. He felt himself instinctively drawing back from the contact of Hitler's hand. The man was obviously mad.

'There is a U-Boat in the area is there not, *Vizeadmiral*?'

'Yes, Fuehrer. *UB-44* is within forty miles or so of Puento Laros.'

'Well? Are not our U-Boats famous for blowing holes in the bottoms of enemy ships – that's what Raeder was telling me earlier today. Or perhaps you do not agree.'

'Of course, but I do not see the connection.'

Hitler sat down with a heavy theatrical sigh. His hands had stopped trembling. He was in full control of himself again and his brain was working with coldly deliberate precision.

'Do you wish me to spell it out for you? I have ordered *Koenig* to be sunk by German hands to avoid the disgrace of seeing her destroyed by the enemy. There is a U-Boat in the area. Then let the U-Boat sink *Koenig*!'

Von Schroeder could scarcely believe his ears. Then he realized that Germany's leader meant every word he was saying. This was *his* idea of a satisfactory solution to an irritating problem. And to maintain his personal authority Hitler intended to ensure that his orders were carried out. No matter by what means!

The Director of Operations could not trust himself to speak. He bowed stiffly, turned on his heel, and walked towards the doors flanked by his two aides.

'A moment, *Herr Vizeadmiral*.'

He stopped at the door and turned. The Fuehrer was leaning forward across the top of his desk like an obscene toad preparing to spring.

'There must be no survivors, von Schroeder,' he said quietly. 'Officially it will be announced that *Koenig* scuttled herself in obedience to my orders. We must therefore ensure that no one escapes to spoil the story. So remember – no survivors.'

As the massive steel doors of the War Room closed behind him von Schroeder had to stop and lean against the wall. He felt physically sick. Then he recovered and returned to the Naval Staff room.

The other officers were equally shocked by Hitler's ruthless order and for a few precarious minutes they discussed the possibility of disobeying. But the moment quickly passed. Discipline reasserted itself and they knew that the instructions, no matter how distasteful, must be carried out. But each member of the Staff was equally anxious to pass the ultimate responsibility for issuing the order to someone else.

Karl Doenitz, as head of the Submarine Branch, was the obvious choice, for all U-Boat operational orders were normally channelled through his headquarters. But frantic telephone calls revealed that the Rear Admiral was, at that moment, flying back to Wilhelmshaven from Berlin. And radio communication on such a delicate matter was impossible.

There was only one way left and von Schroeder took it.

Picking up the telephone he told the operator to connect him to U-Boat HQ at Wilhelmshaven. When he got through he asked to have *Kommodore* Neurath put on the line. As one of the only Party members on the Staff of BDU von Schroeder felt certain that he could be relied upon to carry out the Fuehrer's orders without question.

Neurath's high pitched voice cracked in his ear and he pushed the scrambler switch. He spoke quietly but incisively and took great care to avoid giving a direct order. But he made sure that the *Kommodore* was left in no doubt as to Hitler's intentions.

Von Schroeder felt a heavy weight lift from his shoulders as he replaced the receiver. OKM could not be held responsible if *Koenig* was sunk by a U-Boat. He had merely passed on the Fuehrer's verbal instructions. If a direct order was given to *UB-44* it would have to come from BDU. And the only man who could, and probably *would,* countermand such an order and tell OKM to do its own dirty work, Karl Doenitz, would arrive back in Wilhelmshaven too late to do a damn thing about it.

The art of avoiding responsibility was becoming an important factor in the struggle for survival in Nazi Germany.

CHAPTER TEN

The stalk of *UB-44*'s periscope thrust up into the bright sunlight of Puento Laros Bay exactly fifteen minutes before noon. Hauptmann's navigational skill had been tested to the utmost during the forty mile run to the north. Despite continual course changes and variations in speed he brought the U-boat to within two hundred yards of the point Bergman had selected the previous evening. And for the last ten hours they had remained submerged under the surface, never rising above periscope depth and only then to pick up the mysterious radio signals that the skipper decoded behind guarded curtains in the wardroom.

Rumours were rife – an inevitable consequence when forty men are cramped together in a small confined space with no news of any sort. Most had learned of *Koenig*'s flight to Puento Laros but none guessed the true purpose of *UB-44*'s stealthy underwater drive to the north. Not even Bauer, the First Officer, knew the secret of the cypher messages that hummed into the wireless room every few hours. Whatever it was that was going on it *had* to be big. And the men trusted their commander to see them through.

For Bergman the last ten hours had been a nightmare. Neurath's original signal had been received at 0125 and, from the first, he had felt convinced that there was a transmission error.

BDU to CO UB-44. 0112
Koenig *will sail at 1200 hours in disobedience of the Fuehrer's order. She will be sunk before 1230 hours. There will be no survivors.*

Neurath. Kom.

For a start the tense of the signal puzzled him. How could Neurath predict so confidently 'there will be no survivors'.

No survivors from what? A battle to the death with the blockading British cruisers? Perhaps Berlin had succeeded in getting a saboteur on board while the pocket-battleship lay at anchor licking its wounds – or they knew that *Koenig*'s officers planned to arrest von Mikel and carry out the scuttling order between 1200 and 1230 hours? But why 'no survivors'? And what was the purpose of sending the signal to *UB-44* and no other vessel?

Bergman wrestled with the problem for more than thirty minutes and for the first time in his career he appreciated the olympian loneliness of command. Perhaps if Bauer or Hauptmann read the signal they would be able to make sense of it. But the KK prefix branded it as personal and secret. Not a soul on board *UB-44* must learn its contents. But, worst of all, a lurking doubt as to the meaning of the signal nagged insistently at his brain. But such an interpretation was surely quite impossible. BDU would never order a U-boat commander to carry out such an act.

In desperation Bergman drafted an interrogative signal coded it quickly into KK cypher and handed it to Meister for transmission to Wilhelmshaven via Mexico City.

0420. UB-44 to BDU.

Request clarification of your 0112. Orders not understood. Bergman.

Exactly one hour and forty-seven minutes later Bergman's tightly disciplined little world fell apart as he decoded Neurath's reply.

0539. BDU to CO UB-44

Von Mikel regarded as committing act of mutiny. UB-44 *is to attack and sink* Koenig. *Direct orders from the Fuehrer. There must be no survivors. Repeat* UB-44 *to sink* Koenig. *Neurath. Kom. BDU.*

Bergman looked up at the wardroom clock. It was ten minutes past six. Crumpling the signal into a ball he dropped it in the ash-tray ready for burning but his hand drew back at the last moment as he lowered the lighted match to the paper. His old instincts for self-preservation and survival sounded a sudden warning deep inside his brain. He blew out the match, picked the signal out of the ash-tray and carefully smoothed it flat on the table. One day his life might depend on documentary proof that he had acted in obedience to orders. And that creased and crumped slip of pink paper was all the proof that existed. He was certain that Neurath had not retained a copy for the BDU records.

Picking up the KK code book he placed it back inside the safe. Then, folding the signal into four, he slipped it into a private leather wallet and put it next to the code book. He locked the safe and put the key back in his pocket.

Bergman lifted the telephone and pressed the buzzer to the galley.

'Bring me some black coffee, Heinrich.'

Sitting back on the settee he closed his eyes wearily. He would allow himself three hours to decide. And then, whatever the consequences of that decision, he would act.

Mutiny or murder. They were the stark choices that faced him. To go against the discipline and training that had been instilled into his brain from youth and disobey an order. Or to carry out the Fuehrer's command and destroy his own comrades in an act of cold-blooded premeditated murder.

If Bergman had believed in God he could have prayed. But even this solace was denied him. He had nothing to guide him but his own conscience – and, since meeting Rahel, he was beginning to doubt the validity of his personal moral judgements. Gradually the dilemma resolved itself into a single question. What was best for Germany. And on that score there could be only one answer. Instant and unquestioned obedience to orders.

The decision had been taken and Bergman felt the tension drain from his body. In the final analysis he was nothing more than a coldly calculating killing-machine. And he despised himself.

There was an atmosphere of expectancy in the control

room when he finally emerged from the wardroom and he was conscious of a dozen pairs of eyes trying to read the secrets locked inside his brain. They were about to become trusting accessories to murder. Yet not a single man amongst them knew it.

It was 1143.

'Situation report, Number One.'

The eagerness showed in Bauer's eyes. Like most of the other men aboard *UB-44* he was convinced that they were about to launch an attack on the British cruisers in preparation for *Koenig*'s breakout.

'Last periscope observation at 1100 hours, sir. Visibility good. Force 2 breeze from north-west causing a slight surface swell. The enemy squadron is standing two miles to the north – Hauptmann has been plotting their patrol routine.'

Bergman nodded, walked across to the chart, and glanced down at the triangular course which the Pilot had sketched in with a red pencil. He committed it carefully to memory.

'Up periscope!'

His eye pressed up against the lens as the tube pushed up through the surface. The two cruisers were exactly where Hauptmann had predicted. Swinging his lens towards the mouth of the river he detected a thin column of diesel smoke wafting lazily into the air from behind one of the islands. Von Mikel had obviously brought the pocket-battleship to one-hour notice and was using the diffusers to disperse the exhaust gases. He was puzzled why the British hadn't tried shelling the wounded *Koenig* skulking in her lair. That was how they had destroyed *Konigsburg* in 1914 when she hid herself up the Rufiji River – and she'd been 14 miles inland whereas *Koenig* was lying barely a mile up-river from the estuary.

'Down periscope.'

The answer was obvious. The Royal Navy was playing a desperate bluff. Either they were out of ammunition or their guns were unserviceable. And Rear Admiral Sir Algernon

Blackett-Lloyd, taking a calculated gamble, was patrolling *Koenig's* escape route with two defenceless cruisers hoping to keep von Mikel in the trap until *Hood* and the other heavies came on the scene. If *Koenig,* crippled as she was, came out with all available guns blazing, the Rear Admiral's squadron faced instant destruction.

Not for the first time Bergman experienced a feeling of admiration for the enemy's guts. Centuries of tradition had taught the Royal Navy how to win battles – or to die gloriously if its bluff was called. It was a pity that Hitler and his gold-braided Naval Staff did not have the same appreciation of sea-power's possibilities. The ships were important – and Germany knew how to build good ships. But the men counted for more. And, when the chips were down, it was tradition and leadership that counted. The *Kriegsmarine* had the men – but it was sadly lacking in both tradition and leadership.

He became suddenly aware that the men in the control room were watching him as he stood motionless at the lowered periscope immersed in his thoughts. Mentally shaking himself back to reality he picked up the War Diary and noted the details of his last observations.

'Bow torpedo room stand by !'

'Bow torpedo room secured, sir.'

'Set for fast running – depth 15 feet. Fire a simultaneous salvo when I give you the word.'

He turned to Herzog. The old veteran looked calm and seemed unaffected by the growing tension in the crowded control room. His hands rested lightly on the steel-rimmed wheel as he waited orders.

'Steer 0-3-0, Cox'n.'

'0-3-0, sir.'

'Slow ahead both !'

'Group down – slow ahead both.'

UB-44 began to move forward and nerves started to wind down at the realization that the long hours of waiting were over. The skipper was in command now. There'd soon be some action.

Bergman picked up the microphone of the internal communications system. He knew that he would have to keep it brief or his voice would betray the lies he was about to announce. There was a curious constriction in his throat and he swallowed hard.

'This is the captain. *Koenig* is seriously damaged and the Fuehrer has given orders that she is to be scuttled.' He was conscious of a barely audible groan of disappointment from the men as they heard the announcement. 'Our job is to try and get one – or even both – of the enemy cruisers. It will be a tricky job and every man must carry out his duties with a precision that even I have never demanded from you before. I know you won't let me down.'

The air inside the U-boat was growing stale. Drops of moisture began gathering on the steel bulkheads and chests ached with the effort of breathing. It was an inevitable consequence of being battened down for almost fourteen hours but Bergman knew that it was making the men sluggish. And a man being slowly poisoned by carbon monoxide was not an efficient unit. He nodded to Bauer.

'Release a couple of freshener cartridges in each compartment, Number One. They should just keep the air clear long enough for us to complete our attack.'

Bauer sent a runner forward and another aft with the order and there was a soft hiss of purifying oxygen as the valves were twisted open. It smelled sweetly fresh and the men drew deep refreshing breaths into their clogged lungs.

'Up periscope!'

Bergman took a 30 second sweep from north-west to due west and then ordered the 'scope down again. Von Mikel was on the move. The three mast tips of the pocket-battleship had travelled at least two hundred yards behind the rim of the island since his last observation. And, thank God, he was using the San Domingo channel – the exit farthest away from the enemy cruisers as they dog-legged westwards on their steady relentless triangular beat. Von Mikel had obviously been thinking along the same lines as himself – which was a pity for von Mikel.

What the hell now?

Engineer Veitch had pushed into the control room from the motor room. He was sweating profusely and wiping his face with a wisp of cotton waste.

'Can you hold the manoeuvring down to a minimum, sir. We've located some defective cells in Number Three compartment and we're draining the batteries too fast for comfort.'

'What can you give me?'

'Not more than three amp-hours, sir.* Obviously less if the motors are run at full power.'

'And on full power – what?'

'Thirty minutes – even if we can repair the defective cells and bring them back into the circuit I wouldn't put it at more than one hour.'

Bergman made a quick mental calculation. It might just be enough. But if von Mikel pulled out more than 20 knots, or if he doubled back towards Blackett-Lloyd's cruisers and increased the interception distance, *UB-44* would not have sufficient power to get within torpedo range.

'Nothing to worry about, Chief. Hauptmann's calculations look good. All we have to do is sit and wait for the enemy ships to return.' That's it. Keep up the lies and they'll accept everything you tell them without question. 'I'll have to manoeuvre a little but three amp-hours will be ample.'

Veitch seemed reassured. He hurried back to the motor room to supervise the work of tracing the fault and by-passing the defective cells.

'Do you know how to work the *torpedorechner*, Pilot?'

_____

*A submarine battery's life is limited by the amount of power it can store before recharging. This period is usually expressed in multiples of amp-hours.

179

Hauptmann lifted his head from the charts.

'Yes, sir.'

'Right, I want you to take over from Bauer.' Bergman turned to his First Officer. 'Number One – go up forward and keep an eye on the torpedo tubes. I must have split-second accuracy. We'll be firing all four at once so we'll only get one chance. I can't afford to miss.'

That's killed two cats with one stone. With Hauptmann divorced from his charts and instruments there would be no record of *UB-44*'s guilty track in those last vital thirty minutes. And, in consequence, no evidence of the U-boat's position when the torpedoes were actually fired. Bauer's removal to the bows disposed of another problem. It would not be healthy to have another executive officer in the control room when the time came – especially one as knowledgeable and observant as his First Officer. Any one of a dozen tell-tale signs might betray *UB-44*'s true purpose to an experienced U-Boatman like Bauer. And complete secrecy was vital.

It was not just a case of self-protection, although Bergman had no illusions on that score if anything chanced to go wrong. He wanted to ensure that, in the final analysis, only he as captain could be brought to book for the attack. Although the orders had come from above it remained his responsibility to carry them out. And it was a responsibility he could share with no one else.

'Up periscope!'

The cruisers were still moving westwards and, if Hauptmann's plot was correct, they would be turning in about ten minutes. *Koenig,* too, was gliding forward and as she emerged from behind the sheltered lee of the island he could see her battle damage clearly. Whatever they might say about him in Berlin there was no doubt in Bergman's mind that von Mikel had guts to seek action with such a crippled ship.

'Helm, Port 5 . . . steady . . . midships. Down periscope.'

He walked across to Hauptmann.

180

'Target bearing 020. Range 7,000 yards. Speed 15 knots.'

UB-44's navigator moved the dials of the *torpedorechner* to match the skipper's data. He was too engrossed in his task to notice or remember the subtle change of course.

Herzog, too, crouched robot-like over the helm, sweated with concentration as he held the U-boat on course with the dedication of the true professional. Bergman glanced around at the other men in the control room and saw the same grim determination.

'Up periscope.'

Koenig had cleared the island and was running into the deep water channel. Her bow wave was rising higher this time and Bergman knew that von Mikel was working up to flank speed.

'Target bearing 0-3-0. Range 6,000 yards. Speed 20 knots. What is my aim off?'

Hauptmann's machine clicked furiously as he fed the data into it and Konrad's right foot tapped impatiently.

'DA – Port 10, sir.'

Too much! A deflection angle of that magnitude increased the margin of error to an unacceptable level.

'Full ahead both!' Damn the amp-hours. If he drained the batteries it was too bad. It was win or bust. 'Helmsman steer two points to port . . . steady . . . another point to port . . . midships. Down periscope.'

He stepped back as the column sank softly into its womb.

'Target now bearing 025, Pilot. Range 5,000 yards. Speed 20 knots.'

Not a man in the control room thought to question his intentions. All were convinced that *UB-44* was closing the enemy cruisers and every member of the U-boat's crew were striving to do their best for the captain.

'DA - Port 2,' Hauptmann reported quietly.

'Hydrophone effect clear on bearing Green zero-five, sir,' Schiller called urgently. 'I can't understand it – I could swear I'm picking up diesel engines.'

Hell and damnation! He'd forgotten about the questing ears of the man listening on the hydrophones. And his heart sank as he saw several men in the control room exchanging questioning glances when they heard the report. British cruisers did not use diesel propulsion – but the German Navy did.

Schiller's keen sense of hearing, boosted by the scientific perfection of his listening equipment, gave him the blind man's ability to see in the dark. And, like all good hydrophone operators, he could picture the scene on the surface through his ears almost as accurately as his captain could see it through the periscope lens. What a bloody fool he had been to forget the listening devices.

Bergman lied smoothly and confidently.

'Quite correct, Schiller. There *are* diesel engine sounds in the area – a small American motor coaster is passing between us and the target. That's why I am holding back on our final attack run. It should have passed clear in a few minutes.'

The expressions on the faces of the men in the control room showed that they, at least, had swallowed his glib explanation. And he sighed with inward relief. But Schiller was a skilled professional and he wasn't so easily fooled. At the target range decreased he would quickly realize that the sound throbbing in his ear-phones was being made by the powerful engines of a big ship – not an insignificant coaster. Bergman knew he was skating on the thin ice of credibility but he did not dare risk the chance of further exposure.

He managed to inject an irritated edge to his voice suggestive of raw nerves and growing tension. He snapped rather than spoke.

'Shut those bloody hydrophones off! It's bad enough trying to concentrate in these circumstances without you continually butting in with your misleading reports.'

The skipper was being unreasonable and Schiller knew

it, he could appreciate the stress Bergman was suffering. He removed his earphones obediently and turned the volume control to the left.

Intent on maintaining character Bergman gave a heavy theatrical sigh of relief.

'Group down – half ahead both. Up periscope.'

Now there was only time for a quick glimpse. *Koenig* was still heading for the open sea and their two tracks were closing rapidly. Swinging the lens to the left Bergman saw the British cruisers turning sharply. Von Mikel had been spotted!

'Down periscope . . . target bearing 005. Range 3-five hundred. Speed still 20 knots.'

As Hauptmann fed his machine the Kapitanleutnant made his final preparations for the attack. He wanted *Koenig* moving across his sights from port to starboard and as near broadside-on as possible. An approach shot was easiest and, if his estimate of the range was correct, a hit was certain. But a hit, in itself, was not enough. The pocket-battleship had to be totally destroyed not just sunk. And that meant planting at least one torpedo into her magazine.

'Up periscope!'

Bergman could feel the sweat on his brow as tension built up. The air inside the U-boat was getting stale again and his chest ached with every breath. His eye pressed tightly to the lens as the optical tube broke surface.

'Stop!'

UB-44 was trimmed to a nicety, riding straight and level at precisely thirty feet, and nothing must be allowed to disturb her vital balance. But the slight surface swell caused the waves to break over the periscope lens obscuring his vision. The U-boat was much too close for comfort and the lens periscope showing the better. The only solution was to keep raising and lowering the column a few inches to maintain an unobstructed view of the target.

'Up six inches . . . another two . . . stop. Herzog, I want

you on the hydroplane controls . . . Second Coxswain?

'Sir?'

'Take over the helm from Herzog. Steer one point to starboard – standard course is 0-3-0.'

'0-3-0 standard sir. Steer one point to starboard.'

The attack position was developing nicely. *Koenig,* anxious to break clear as fast as possible, was holding a straight course and *UB-44*'s bows were virtually at right angles to her unsuspecting target.

'Drop her a couple of inches . . . that's it. Hold it there.'

The sea quickly drained from the angled protective glass covering the lens and Bergman rubbed the eye-piece objective with a soft anti-static cloth. Twisting the periscope to the left he focussed on the cruisers. They had wheeled around in a sharp about-turn when *Koenig*'s escape had been spotted and black smoke was belching from their funnels as they settled down to a long stern chase. He could imagine the frantic signals being flashed from the enemy's radio-sets as they called for assistance.

The lowered position of the periscope meant that he had to hunch his body awkwardly to see through the eye-piece and his shoulders were aching. But personal discomfort was the last thing in his mind now.

'Target bearing 0-3-0. Range 2000. Speed 20 knots. Stand-by torpedo room. Check depth and setting please.'

Bauer's voice, oddly metallic as it came through the loud-speaker grille in the control room, reported back.

'Fast speed setting – running depth 15 feet. Ready for salvo firing, sir.'

Bergman thought quickly. He began to wish that he had staggered the depth settings. But it was too late for second thoughts now. Only a minute or so to go and there was no time to draw the torpedoes and adjust the depth-keeping hydrostatic valves.

'Flood up tubes.'

Torpedomechaniker Heindecker pulled the lever to open

the outer doors of the torpedo tubes and *UB-44's* bows dipped slightly with the increased weight of water. But Herzog was ready. Watching his controls like an eagle he blew water from Number 12 tank to compensate and restore trim – and then shut off the air at the precise moment the U-boat came level.

'Good work, Cox'n.'

Bergman watched the graceful *panzerschiffe* coming into his sights and he searched along the grey painted side for the scuttle-less section that identified the location of the magazines. His experienced eye detected an increase in speed as *Koenig's* engineers managed to screw an extra two knots from their battle-strained engines and he saw the attack angle suddenly narrow.

'Stop port motor. Half ahead starboard.'

PB-44's bows pivoted in line with the target like a matador circling a bull. Bergman let her draw slightly ahead.

'Full ahead both.'

Squatting down in the bows of the U-boat Heindecker turned the levered taps of the tubes in sequence and quickly shut them off again as a jet of water shot from each. He nodded to Bauer standing behind him at the internal telephone.

'Bow tubes flooded up, sir.'

'Stand by.' Bergman switched to the high-power attack lens for the final moments. He could see *Koenig* large and clear, a mountain of steel, crashing through the sea like a snow-plough on a mountain pass. He could even see the heads of the officers standing behind the shattered glass windows of the shell-scarred bridge. And he suddenly remembered the last time he had seen *Koenig* – that late summer's day in August when the world was still at peace – his fears that von Mikel would report him to Doenitz for making an insubordinate signal.

And, ironically, his final message – *Auf Wiedersehen*.

The sharp-cut bows cleaved past the centre aiming-line

185

of the periscope's sights and Bergman's hands tightened on the steering handles as he watched the long line of fo'c'sle scuttles glide across the lens. He was surprised that he felt so calm. Did all murderers experience this strange feeling of detachment as they surveyed their defenceless victims with the knife poised in their hands.

The long row of scuttles stopped abruptly and the smooth skin of the armoured belt shielding the magazines above the waterline centred in his sights. This time it really was *auf Wiedersehen, Koenig*!

'Fire!'

UB-44 lurched as all four torpedoes shot from the tubes and spread in a four fingered salvo towards the target.

It was too late now. He was fully committed. Once launched on their lethal way nothing could call the torpedoes back — the die was cast. Fascinated with horror at the act of murder he had perpetrated Bergman stayed glued to the periscope. The electric motors of the *Type G-7e* torpedoes left almost no visible track on the surface and he had no way of knowing whether they were running true or wild. Mechanically he counted off the seconds.

Suddenly he wrenched away from the periscope.

'We've missed,' he announced flatly. 'The only chance we had and we missed.'

There was a murmur of disappointment from the men grouped together in the control room. Hauptmann snapped his pencil in disgust and Neisser, the Second Coxswain, began to swear quietly, comprehensively, and methodically. Bergman leaned against the chart table, hands thrust deeply into his pockets, staring at the floor despondently. Yet, outwardly dejected, his mind remained alert and he continued the mental count-down: *Fifty-nine . . . sixty . . . sixty-one*.

Herzog was the only man in the control room who did not join in the general murmur of disappointment. His face was expressionless as he stared up at the inclometer. Like the skipper he was counting as well.

Bergman pushed himself away from the chart-table with his hips, walked to the periscope, and pulled the microphone down to mouth level.

'This is the captain. The attack has failed. (*seventy-three . . . seventy-four . . .*) Every member of the crew did his job well and no one is to blame. So far as I could see the magnetic fuzes on the torpedoes were faulty . . .'

A reverberating detonation interrupted his announcement. It was followed immediately by a thunderclap explosion that echoed through the submarine and threw *UB-44* sideways as the pressure wave created by the concussion hit her. The lights went out and men reeled and fell in the sudden darkness. Bergman picked himself up from the floor as the emergency lighting flickered to life. Exactly eighty seconds. His calculations had been correct to the last second. Grasping the handles of the periscope he peered through the lens.

The sea was empty.

Koenig had disappeared in a single split-second flash as her magazines ignited. All that marked her grave was a widening circle of oil from her shattered fuel tanks and a few pathetic scraps of wreckage. A spreading mushroom cloud of brownish smoke hung silently in the air above the spot where she had vanished like a funeral pall.

Bergman searched the surface of the sea with the high-magnification attack lens but there was no sign of life. Not a single soul had survived the cataclysmic explosion which *UB-44*'s torpedoes had triggered. He felt suddenly sick as he viewed the destruction he had caused.

'Half speed both.' His voice sounded strangely normal. 'Take her to 100 feet, Cox'n. Helmsman, reverse course . . . steer 2-1-0.'

His hands were trembling as he reached for the microphone again. This was the worst moment of all. But, if he didn't make the announcement here and now, he knew he would never make it at all. With his throat already closing with nervous reaction Bergman forced himself to speak.

'This is the captain . . . Kapitan von Mikel has carried out the Fuehrer's orders. *Koenig* has been scuttled and the enemy has been deprived of victory.' He hesitated as he groped for the right words. 'I think something may have gone wrong with the scuttling plan. So far as I could see through the periscope *Koenig*'s magazines ignited and she was blown to pieces . . . there appear to be no survivors.'

Bergman hung the microphone back on its hook alongside the periscope. *UB-44*, still operating under emergency lighting, was a vault of gloomy silence as the men assimilated the news. Yet they seemed to have accepted his account of *Koenig*'s demise as being the truth. And, for their sake, he was glad.

Bauer came aft from the torpedo compartment. He looked tired, disappointed, and despondent.

'Could we surface, sir?' he asked. 'We might find some poor devils hanging on to the wreckage.'

Bergman thought of the glutinous blanket of oil that marked the pocket-battleship's final resting-place. Even if, by some miracle, anyone had lived through the explosion, they would not last two minutes in that muck. He shook his head.

'Sorry, Number One, but we must remain submerged and stay out of sight.' He forced a laugh. 'If the British knew there was a U-boat within a thousand miles of this place Churchill would be telling the world that a German submarine had sunk the *Koenig*. You remember how they blamed us for sinking the *Athenia*? The British Admiralty can be convincing liars.'

The men smiled grimly at his macabre joke. Only one man in the control room did not join in their amusement. He sat stolid and silent, with his back towards them, gripping the polished rim of the hydroplane operating wheel. Suddenly he swung round.

He said nothing. But Bergman could read the hatred in the Coxswain's eyes. And, at that precise moment, he knew

188

that Herzog shared his guilty secret. Years of experience had given the old veteran an uncanny knowledge of U-boats and underwater warfare. And he was no fool. He could remember the last target range which Bergman had called off to Hauptmann and he had counted the seconds it would take a 45-knot torpedo to travel that distance. The explosion of *Koenig*'s magazines had coincided precisely with his estimate of the elapsed time necessary to obtain a hit.

An angry hate gnawed at Herzog's guts. This was the man who had befriended him – who had found him a billet in an operational U-boat when he had been over age for combat duties. The man he had respected and admired. And he was no more than another Nazi thug.

As he sat at the planesman's seat staring at *Kapitanleutnant* Konrad Siegfried Bergman the Coxswain swore a silent oath to serve at his side until Germany could repay her debt to him for the murder of 1,000 innocent German sailors.

The news of *Koenig*'s destruction reached Berlin during the night of 12 January, 1940, and the Fuehrer was informed by his Naval ADC at breakfast. He accepted the information with a casual disinterested shrug. His only satisfaction lay in the knowledge that *he* had exacted obedience from the Navy where Raeder had failed.

Later that morning he summoned the Naval ADC back to the War Room where he was studying the OKM appraisal of his latest brain-child, Exercise Weser.* *Kapitan* Ritter von Schoen entered into the Fuehrer's presence, saluted smartly, and removed his cap. Hitler looked up from the files that scattered across his desk.

'Good morning, Schoen. Tell me – the U-Boat that carried out my order regarding the *Koenig* . . .'

'*UB-44*, mein Fuehrer?'

*Exercise Weser – *Weserübung* – was the operational code name given to the projected German invasion of Norway and Denmark.

'Yes, that is the one. What is the name of her commander?'

'Bergman, Fuehrer. Kapitanleutnant Bergman.'

Hitler repeated the name to himself quietly as if committing it to memory. He sat back in his chair with his hands clasped.

'He is a young man who needs watching, von Schoen. It is a pity that the circumstances will not permit public recognition of his achievement. But, and mark my words well, we must keep a very close eye on him in the future.'

The Fuehrer's intuitive warning of danger was not misplaced. Any man with the strength of purpose to kill a thousand of his fellow-countrymen in blind obedience to an order was a man to be feared. Such a man was equally capable of destroying the very system that had produced him if the bonds of discipline were broken and the dictates of conscience took their place.

Kapitanleutnant Bergman was, indeed, a very dangerous man.

THE END

SPIES, INTRIGUE, ADVENTURE— THE BEST READING FROM PINNACLE BOOKS!

BOMB RUN, by Spencer Dunmore. An excitingly written story about a bomb run over Berlin in 1944, the thirtieth and final mission for one British Bomber Command air crew. They will take off tonight, make a last passage through the barrage of flak and flame, take a last gamble against the Messerschmitts, and return to England and relative peace. But across the Channel, a young German fighter pilot, grieving for his dead parents and thinking of the combat to come, is destined to alter forever the lives of the bomber pilot and his crew. A thrilling and compelling novel.**P116—95¢**

SABERLEGS, by Eric Pace. An incredible tale of intrigue, woven by one of the *New York Times'* top foreign correspondents, as scaringly possible as it is exciting. The mission of Charles Randall: to get Von Zugen, the sadistic German scientist who invented a lethal weapon for Hitler, escaped with it at the war's end, and now wants to sell it to Arab commandos for use against Israel. A story taut with suspense and tender with half-realized love—a brilliantly constructed spy novel.

P061—95¢

OVER THE WALL, by Duncan Thorp. A suspenseful adventure of revolution and assassination. There are only six people in the group—one a woman—who plan to ignite the take-over of a Caribbean island. They are up against a brutal and powerful dictator whose rule has been absolute and impregnable. The fight for leadership among the six is almost as exciting and intriguing as the revolution they foment. Romance, sex and action for the most demanding adventure aficionado!

P101—95¢

THE ELECTION, by Sherwin Markman. What happens when an exciting presidential election is tied, and the final decision is thrown into the House of Representatives. Heightening the complications and tensions, too, are the simultaneous riots of black militants across the country. America is in chaos! The pivotal figure in this melee is Stu Brady, a young assistant press secretary. Stu becomes the liaison man between the major candidates, as scandal and intrigue come to the boiling point. An election you'll never forget!   **P100—$1.50**

CLASH OF DISTANT THUNDER, by A. C. Marin. A spy story you'll find difficult to put down; impossible to forget. The spy, Dr. John Wells. His assignment, to find a missing informant in Paris. This misplaced agent may have defected or may have been a double agent right along. Or he may have been loyal—but has been caught and silenced. Wells is the hunted as well as the hunter, from Paris to Switzerland and Italy. A wild chase of shadows and suspense.   **P064—95¢**